Title: The Unwilling Bridge
Subtitle: Collection Book for Hot Romance Short Stories
Author: Adrienne Cotton

From the Publisher:
Thank you for purchasing this book.

Table of Contents

A Beautiful Western Dream

Description

Daisy Hatfield has always been the golden daughter of her family and is very loved by her small town, Allendale, Texas. She loves sewing clothes and hopes to open her fashion brand when she can. However, she realizes that she can't afford the luxury yet as the firstborn daughter of sheepherders. So Daisy takes care of their home without complaint.

However, on her thirtieth birthday, Daisy receives news that threatens to turn over everything she believes in.

She is to be betrothed to Richard Branson, a wealthy horse racer in New Orleans.

Weary by this news, Daisy reluctantly agrees to this arrangement because she realizes it'll help her family financially.

Moving away from her small home, Daisy has no idea what is coming her way or who the man she's supposed to marry will be.

Richard only agrees to take a wife so his family would get off his back. However, he realizes that his father had already picked out his wife and has no choice but to adhere to the agreement, so he doesn't lose his inheritance.

Determined to keep Daisy at arm's length, Richard maintains a cold demeanor towards her.

How long do will this energy keep going on between these two? And will be able to achieve her long-term dream?

Chapter 1

"Oh Daisy, you outdid yourself with this one." Lisa Hatfield gasped as she twirled in the dress her sister made for her. Her eyes shone when she noticed the pockets in the sides of the dress – practical for a farm girl.

Daisy Hatfield smiled at her younger sister and shrugged. "Happy birthday again. I hope you really like it."

"What? I *love* it." Lisa looked at her reflection in the mirror. Daisy knew that Lisa was a much younger version of herself. They had the same oval face, blue eyes, and long untamed blond hair.

The dress she had made for Lisa was perfectly matched with her pale skin. The dress was an ocean blue color with a high collar and a diamond cut right into the chest area. The bodice was slim on Lisa's thin frame but fanned out at knee length. Now she had a pretty dress for the coming Sunday.

Daisy lifted the dress and grinned. "I think this is my favorite part." She was referring to the pants sewn to the dress. The skirt was detachable, and she could show off the pants instead. Perfect for Lisa to keep being the tomboy she was.

"Mine too."

Daisy peeped out the window. Their mother had noticed they were gone and was already looking around for them. "Come on; mama will soon call for us. Let's go." Their mother would frown on Daisy using her savings to buy materials so she could sew, so she tried to hide them from her. She doubted she could really fool her mother. Martha Hatfield was a very smart woman.

Lisa quickly removed the dress and delicately folded it into her locker before putting on her dungarees.

They both climbed down the wooden stairs that creaked with age and made their way to the backyard.

Jingles, their cow, mooed as soon she saw Daisy. The milking of the cow had been done by Daisy ever since she was little, and Jingles had been their cow for years. She had given birth to tiny calves that were still too young to be used for anything.

"Jingles has been waiting for you." Martha frowned, the lines in her forehead etching deeply. Martha was a strong-looking woman, and Daisy meant that literally. She had muscles in her arms and a vein ticked in her forehead.

Daisy had seen younger pictures of her mother and knew how beautiful she was when she was younger. Way before their father died and left them with crippling debt.

Martha had paid it all, but she had to keep a household of six running. It was taking a toll on her, and Daisy could see.

Daisy bit her lip with guilt. She was 28 and had told her mother she wanted to go to the city to look for a job, but Martha had disagreed with her. She said Daisy couldn't survive in 'that big place where everyone loses their soul. You stay here and take care of the home and your siblings.'

Daisy didn't argue further. Truth be said, she wanted to help, but at the same time, she didn't think she was ready for a large and busy place.

Daisy wiped her hands on her apron and made her way to Jingles.

The cow looked at her with dark eyes and looked away with disinterest. It was a routine they had done over and over again. Daisy sat on the small wooden stool and got to work. She milked the cow's udder while whispering soft words to her. Soon enough, they were done.

Daisy covered the large bucket of milk and set it aside. Her younger brothers, Jack and Aiden had been given the task to skim the milk.

"Come on Daisy, let's set out the meal. The guests should start arriving soon." Daisy glanced up at the sound of her mother's voice.

She knew they were having guests, but Daisy had no idea who they were. Every time she asked her mother, she was met with tight lips and skittish movements. So Daisy decided to let it go.

"Coming," Daisy said as she walked into the house through the backdoor. Their house was an old thing that looked like it was going to fall over anytime soon. Surprisingly, it had not in the twenty-eight years that Daisy had been living there.

She was the first child, and only she and her twenty-two-year-old brother Jack remembered what their father was like.

Daisy was fourteen when he died, but she remembered him to be jovial and taught them many tricks. Of course, that was when he wasn't drunk.

When he had died, Daisy had cried as she was supposed to, but she barely had any time to grieve her father. Martha refused to let anyone slack, and almost immediately, Daisy had to shoulder a lot of burdens.

Her mother sold their farm produce at the farmers' market, and she was left with running the house. It was hard enough taking care of the house, but to combine it with raising four siblings, Daisy barely had any time for herself.

She tried her best to patch up the house to look nice. She had sewn together old fabrics to make quilts. She used colorful pieces of cloth to cover the torn parts of the couch and the curtains.

Daisy walked up to her mother in the kitchen. There was a rotting avocado on the table, and she picked it up to throw into the dustbin.

Martha was slicing some tomatoes and stirring something that smelled delicious in the pot.

Daisy raised her brows when she saw her. Martha was wearing a flowery dress, and her salt and pepper hair was put into a low bun. It was better than her usual tight ponytail. She had cleaned up nicely.

"Wow, mama, it looks like this guest is a special person," Daisy said with a teasing tone as she threw a bit of sausage into her mouth when she thought her mother wasn't looking.

"It's really not what you think." Martha avoided her gaze and poured the diced tomato into the cooking pot.

Daisy opened her mouth to ask more, but Martha shook her hand. "You need to get dressed. Wear your Sunday dress. And you should put your hair down, or else it'll grow stiff and fall off. Let it down today."

Daisy cocked her curiously. She had never had to dress up for anyone unless it was to show them the dresses she had sewn.

Still, she didn't ask questions. She decided to do what she was asked.

"Hey Daisy, we are done." Drew, the youngest of them, walked up to her with a bounce to his steps.

Ever since Drew hit puberty, he had been pulsing with nervous energy, and his gangly limbs always seemed to move on their own. Regardless, he was her favorite sibling, but she would never tell anyone that.

"Hey, Drew, Drew. Okay, just put it in the freezer like always. I'll be sure to work on it later."

Drew nodded and hopped off. Daisy chuckled as she watched his receding figure. Then she turned and climbed the stairs leading to her room.

The room was a storage that had to be turned into a bedroom as their home expanded and money became tighter.

Daisy did what she could do with the room and had hung a yellow curtain she had sewn years ago. It was worn out, but it still served its purpose.

There was a bunk bed right in the middle of the room. She had the lower bunk, and Lisa took the top bunk. There wasn't much else other than a cupboard and a mirror.

Daisy opened the cupboard that served as a wardrobe and pulled out a folded dress. It was almost like the one she had sewn for Leslie, except it was a light pink color and the materials were more flowy. The skirt had ruffles in it and gave it the illusion of being breezy even though there was no draft in the house.

It was one of her favorite words, and this will be the first time she'll be wearing it.

She had applied to a fashion school in New Orleans using the neighbor's laptop, but Daisy didn't expect anything from it. So she didn't keep her hopes up.

Daisy laid it out on her bed and took a quick shower in the bathroom. She had to shower cold so her siblings could make use of the hot water.

She sighed when she looked at her reflection in the mirror. Her hair and water were always at war with each other.

Her curly blond hair was standing on end, and she knew she would have to spend quite a while on it so that she could tame it.

Daisy toweled herself dry and wore the dress she had laid out. She quickly set to work and put a hairbrush on her hair.

A few minutes in, Lisa came running into the room. She was panting, and Daisy stared at her, bewildered.

"Why are you running as if you are being chased?"

Lisa shook her head and straightened, trying to catch her breath. "The guests... I think they are here. I just saw a car headed our way. Not just any car, I think it's the new car they keep advertising on TV. Come, look outside."

Daisy set down her brush and allowed Lisa to drag her to the window. True to her words, an expensive-looking car headed their way. It had almost reached the front of their farmhouse.

She closed the windows and knew she had to be ready before her mother called for her. Lisa dashed off to take a quick shower, and Daisy finished brushing her hair.

Finally, it was docile enough to be pulled into a low ponytail. Daisy rubbed a bit of talc on her face and stood up, ready to go downstairs.

She heard chattering outside and knew her mother had gone to welcome the guests. Maybe they were distant relatives.

She smoothened out her dress and slipped her feet into sandals before making her way down the stairs.

The first thing Daisy noticed were the two main ones who seemed to fill out their tiny living room. She stopped in her steps. The first man was an older person, and he looked to be in his late seventies. He wore a tailored suit with a gold walking stick in his left hand.

Daisy saw how he looked at her and smiled genuinely. She wondered if she knew him.

The second man... now that caught Daisy off-guard. Being from a small town like Allendale, the men around her were the ones she had grown up with. They paled in comparison beside the man standing in their living room.

He was tall. That was the first thing she noticed. Daisy was only 5'3, and she wondered how tiny she would look beside the man. He had dark hair cropped close to his scalp, but somehow it looked good on him. His face seemed like it had been sculpted from a rock and his unsmiling face did nothing to dampen that thought.

He was ridiculously handsome, and Daisy wondered how her mother had come to know these men.

He wore an emerald suit that looked like it had been made solely for him.

Almost like he could feel Daisy staring, he turned to look at her. His grey eyes pierced through her, and he looked away with disinterest.

Martha beckoned to Daisy. "Come here. This is Daisy, my first daughter." She said it as if she was merely doing that for pleasantries.

The older man looked like he had heard about her, and his next words confirmed that. "Daisy, it's nice to meet you finally. I've heard a lot about you."

Daisy smiled shyly and warily. She glanced at her mother, hoping for some introduction, but Martha only looked away and called out for the rest of her siblings.

Soon enough, they were all settled on the dining table, and Martha arranged food on the table. Daisy couldn't remember the last time she saw that much food in their home. There was even dessert, which was ice cream that Daisy herself. Had made.

The older man took upon himself to ask about everyone. The younger man silently ate his food. It was almost like he wasn't there, yet all Daisy could feel was his presence.

Her siblings were delighted to have that much food and made sure to eat as much as they could stuff in their frames.

Almost as if Martha realized she couldn't stall anymore, she cleared her throat and looked around. "Kids, please excuse us. Daisy, you stay."

They all looked at each other, wondering what was going on, but soon enough, it was just Daisy with the two men and her mother.

Finally, she summoned courage and spoke. "Mom, what is going on?"

Her mother's mouth quivered, and that alarmed Daisy. In all the years that she had been alive, she had never seen her mother display any form of weakness until now.

Martha grabbed Daisy's hands tightly. "You will be going with them."

Daisy looked at the men and back at her mother. She was confused. "I don't understand."

The older man cleared his throat and spoke. His eyes were serious. "I am aware your mother hasn't told you, despite me telling her you should have known beforehand. Still, the time is now. I'm Owen Branson, and this is my son, Richard Branson. You are betrothed to him."

The first thing that came to Daisy's mind was to laugh. She let out a high pitch laugh, and it was when she saw the alarmed look on her mother's face that she realized this wasn't a joke after all.

Daisy slowly looked at Richard. He didn't look surprised by any of it and only fixed his gaze on Daisy, almost like he was waiting for her reaction.

"Mom, what the hell is this?" Daisy stood up in an outburst. "Is this some terrible prank? Or punishment? When did I get betrothed to him? Answer me!"

Martha's eyes filled with tears. "It's all your father's fault. He left us with such crippling debt that I had no choice but to turn to Mr. Branson Sr. I'm sorry, Daisy, but we struck a deal there and then. I was desperate and too afraid to let you know."

Daisy's hands shook as she heard this. She said quietly, "How can you send me to a man I don't know? What if he's a—"

Martha shook her head. "I would never put you in the wrong hands. Plus, it's only an arranged marriage. You have to be a wife in practice. All you have to do is stay in the same house. Richard needs a little bit of credibility, and we need the money. Daisy, please do this for us."

Daisy looked at her mother and couldn't believe what she was hearing. She sat down and said coldly. "I'll go, but I don't want to have anything to do with you again, Ma."

Martha choked and shut her eyes, and tears rolled down her face, but she didn't say anything.

Owen looked forlorn but didn't say anything. Richard's face was religiously blank.

Daisy sat down and asked, "When do I leave?"

Richard responded. "Tomorrow."

Daisy nodded. So they had already planned all of it. "If I am to go with you, then I want to do it on my terms. As long as I am there, I want my family to live the best life. I want them to go back to school."

Richard looked at her with his dark eyes. He could be likened to a statue as he barely displayed any emotions and said little. "Done."

Daisy didn't say anything as she stood up and left the table. It was when she climbed up the stairs that she let out a shaky breath. As soon as she turned to the passage leading to her room, Daisy was startled to see her siblings all hurdled in the corner.

Lisa ran to her with tears in her eyes. "Please don't go. I'll beg, mama."

The tears Daisy had been holding back streamed down her face. "I'm sorry. I'll come visiting often." She hadn't asked where they were moving to simply because she couldn't bear to find out how far away she would be.

Jack squeezed her arm. She could see that he was fighting back the tears and all that he did was make Daisy cry harder.

She pulled them all into a hug and whispered comforting words to them. "I'll never leave you alone. At least now, you will have a life worth living. I want you to be happy."

That night, as Daisy laid down and closed her eyes, she dreamt of strange men and cages.

Chapter 2

The next morning, Daisy woke up before dawn broke. She didn't need her mother to wake her up as she packed her belongings into a box. She didn't have much to take, and she stared wistfully at her sewing machine. She wished she could take it with her, but it was too heavy to carry anyway.

She turned to say goodbye to Lisa but found that the bed was empty. So she assumed her sister had gone to the toilet.

Daisy wore a grey dress that matched perfectly with her mood. She didn't think she had to impress anyone, so she simply put on the most boring cloth ever.

Her siblings were downstairs waiting for her as soon as she walked into the living room, clutching a suitcase.

Her brothers, Drew and Aiden, hugged her first. Aiden wasn't much of a talker in the house, so he surprised her when he looked at her with his big brown eyes and said, "I will miss you. I hope you come back soon."

Daisy kissed his forehead. He was already taller than her, so she stood on her tiptoes. "I will be back, I promise. Take care of yourself, okay? And help around the house. Also, prepare to go back to school, all of you."

After they had exchanged tight hugs and shed a few tears, Daisy was ready to leave the house she had known all her life.

Martha walked her out of the house to where the car was waiting. It seemed they had slept at a nearby hotel and had gotten to their house early.

"Before you go." Martha sniffed as she looked at Daisy with red eyes. It looked like she had barely gotten any sleep and had aged overnight. "I just want you to know that I would die first before putting you at risk. Please, be happy."

Daisy didn't reply because she just couldn't. Her throat was choked up, and she knew if she opened her mouth to speak, she'd simply burst into tears. Still, she couldn't bring herself to speak to her mother. There was anger brewing in her chest.

Daisy walked past her mother and up to the car. She turned to look at the house and saw her siblings hurdled together, staring at her from the door frame. She waved weekly at them and finally got into the car.

There was a driver that Daisy hadn't noticed they had come with, and Owen occupied the seat right beside him.

Richard sat in the backseat, and Daisy knew she would sit right beside him. She sat close to the door.

"You better sit well. It's going to be a long journey. I won't bite you," Richard said with his eyes closed.

Daisy adjusted a bit and felt her face burn up. She stole glances at him and wondered what he needed the credibility for. Surely, he wasn't a murderer, was he? Fear seized her heart, and Daisy swallowed as the car drove away and the farmhouse became smaller.

"Where are we going?" she asked in a small voice.

Owen turned back and gave her a reassuring smile. "New Orleans."

Daisy stood up, alarmed. New Orleans was like an entire world away. How would she adjust to such a lifestyle? She kept her thoughts to herself and watched them speed past the familiar buildings she was leaving behind.

The car ride was calm other than the music coming from the radio. Owen seemed to be typing away at his phone, and Michael closed his eyes all through. It looked like he was asleep.

Daisy couldn't help but notice how relaxed his face was when he was asleep. His face looked softer, and he didn't look as cold as before. Maybe she could learn to tolerate him till whatever problem he was in passed away.

She wondered how being married could change that problem. It was odd to her.

Soon enough, she found herself dozing off as the hum of the air conditioner put her to sleep. Her eyes became too heavy to open, and Daisy fell into a restless sleep.

*****

Daisy snuggled into the hard pillow she had her head-on. It was hard, but she found it oddly comforting.

She felt a tap on her shoulder and tried to shake it off. All she wanted to do was sleep. She was so tired...

"Hey, we are here."

Daisy's eyes flew open at the proximity of Richard's voice. She was horrified to find out that she had fallen asleep on him. His chest was the hard pillow.

Her face turned red when she saw the amusement in his eyes. Daisy turned away from him and fumbled with the door, trying to get down.

Richard reached across her, his expensive perfume drifting up to her nose, and unlocked the door so she could open it.

Daisy let out a deep breath in an attempt to calm her racing heart.

"Finally." Owen stretched and adjusted his suit. He turned to Daisy with kind eyes. "I hope you are hungry."

On cue, Daisy's stomach rumbled with hunger. She hadn't eaten since the last dinner they had had, and now it was almost noon.

She turned around to look at where they were. They were at the airport, which was a town away from Allendale. Her beloved town didn't have an airport, only a ferry station, so they had to travel just to get to the nearest airport.

They walked to a section of the airport, and a lone airplane stood right in the middle of the takeoff field.

Owen smiled at her. "That's ours. Come on."

Daisy blinked. So they owned an entire airplane? She didn't have time to think about it because they were all climbing up the stairs leading to the airplane.

The interior of the airplane screamed of luxury. There were individual chairs that looked so comfortable, and Daisy immediately sat in one. It was so soft she almost sank into the chair.

An air hostess walked up to her with a beaming smile. "Welcome on board. I'm Anita; what would you like to have?"

Daisy shook her head silently.

Owen laughed. "Oh please, get the lady the finest food you have. I'll have my usual liquor."

Anita nodded and turned to Richard, who had his eyes closed. Daisy watched Anita adjust her top to reveal a bit of cleavage as she batted her eyelashes at him. "And what would you like, sir?"

"I'm good," Richard said gruffly. "You can leave."

Anita was taken aback by the rejection but quickly recovered and walked away.

Daisy stared at Richard as he closed his eyes and leaned into his seat. She admired what kind of person he was.

"Are you going to keep staring? Don't worry, you'll do enough of that."

Daisy was startled with horror as she realized Richard had caught her watching. She quickly looked away and stared out of the window at the thick white clouds that surrounded them.

Thankfully, they didn't waste any time, and a large food tray was placed on a stool right in front of Daisy.

There was lobster, cream cheese, Apple pie, and a variety of foods she hadn't dreamt of ever tasting. She gingerly picked up a piece of lobster and put it into her mouth.

The tastes exploded on Daisy's tongue, and she closed her eyes with satisfaction.

Realizing her hunger was going to win over her shame, Daisy ate as much as she could, and when she was full, they took the plate away.

She stared mournfully at the leftovers and wished her siblings could have a taste of what she had just eaten.

The rest of the flight was quiet, with the pilot updating them on their location, the hostess asking whether they were okay and Daisy drifting in and out of sleep.

She opened her eyes and looked out the window, and that was when she knew that they had reached New Orleans.

The city was totally lit up, and the sun had set, so it looked like something from a Hollywood movie.

They all got down from the airplane, and immediately Daisy got down, she knew that she was in a different place.

The air smelt different and wasn't as fresh as back home. Also, there was a limousine waiting for them.

Richard stretched and walked directly to the Limousine. Daisy waited for Owen to follow, but he stayed back.

He saw that she had noticed and shook her head. "I won't be going with you. But here's my card. I'm aware you don't have a cellphone, which will be arranged as soon as you get home. I'll come to see you from time to time." He moved closer and squeezed her arm. "I promise you will be safe. You don't have to worry about anything."

Daisy swallowed and nodded. This was it. She turned to look at the limo. Richard had gotten in already, so she followed suit and climbed into the vehicle.

Now it was just the two of them in the space, and Daisy squirmed awkwardly. She knew that the time would come, but now that it was here, she wasn't sure if she was to speak or not.

Richard opened a bottle of liquor and poured it into a cup. He offered it to Daisy, but she shook her head.

Richard downed the glass and set it on a nearby counter. Daisy looked away, blinking rapidly, and stared at a hole in the chair.

"You can leave if you want."

Daisy thought she hadn't heard right. "Huh?"

Richard stretched out in his seat. "You can leave if you want."

Daisy couldn't believe the opportunity appeared on a platter of gold. Still, she hesitated before taking it.

Summoning courage, she asked, "Why do you need a wife?"

Richard rocked his head side to side. "Not necessarily a woman, but... here's why." He clicked on a few tabs on his phone and handed it to her.

It was a video, and Daisy began playing it. She could see a race field or something like it, and then she saw Richard. He was running towards a man, and Daisy gasped when she saw him punch the man.

He didn't stop there; he kept punching him until some men dragged him away.

Daisy shook as the video ended. How could she live with such a violent man? She handed him back his phone and swallowed.

"So I got suspended for that. I could have been banned for life, but I guess they decided not to. As long as I get my life together or act as I do, I'm all good. What greater way to prove that than to get a wife?"

"Why did you hit him?"

Richard looked at her with his grey eyes. Eyes that swam with many secrets. "He insulted my mother."

Daisy had been expecting him to say something else, but not that. "Oh."

Richard closed his eyes. "Yeah. Like I said, you can leave."

Daisy thought about it. Her staying here meant a better life for her siblings. Also, deep down, she was glad she was leaving home, even though it was in an unconventional way. "How long do we have to be together?"

"Three months."

Daisy nodded and swallowed. "I'll stay."

Richard was surprised. He had expected her to take him on his offer. He nodded and glanced away. "Alright."

The rest of the car ride was very quiet, and soon enough, they pulled up in front of a hotel.

That was what Daisy thought before the driver said, "Welcome home."

She got down from the car and clutched her suitcase in her hand. The sight before her froze her to the ground.

The house was huge. No, huge was undermining the massive mansion that stood right in front of her.

It was a tall grey house with a large driveway that could double as a soccer field.

There was a fountain right in the middle of the compound with a golden statue spewing water out of its mouth.

There were golden pillars right beside the doorway leading to the house, each arching above the door with angels perched on them.

Richard arched an eyebrow at her, and Daisy was finally able to move. Immediately, an older woman in an apron came to meet them. She was followed by a person that Daisy assumed to be the butler.

The butler collected her suitcase from her before bowing down.

The older woman had rose plump cheeks that paired perfectly with her round figure. "Oh, welcome sir." She turned to Daisy and gave her a small smile before bowing. "You must be the Miss. Welcome. This is your new home."

Daisy was appalled by the display of extravagant courtesy and could only mumble incoherently.

The butler carried her bag and opened the door, waiting for her to walk in.

Daisy staggered at the vast amount of space. The inside of the house could easily be mistaken as a cathedral as the ceiling way far up with chandeliers hanging from it.

A shelf with various awards and plagues was displayed as soon as they walked into the room, and Daisy was amazed by the marble walls.

The furniture was made of leather, and the color-matched perfectly with the curtains that hung from the large French windows.

An unlit fireplace was built in the corner, and more plagues were placed on the mantle.

Daisy felt like she was in the middle of an interior magazine.

Richard immediately walked away from them, and the older woman turned to look at Daisy.

"My name is Wanda, and I'll be showing you to your room."

Daisy followed Wanda as they climbed up the spiral stairs with gold handles. They turned into a corridor with rows and rows of rooms lined by each other.

"There's Master's room." Martha pointed at the first oak door. "And there's yours." She pointed to the door opposite Richard's.

She turned the key to the door and pushed it open.

The scent of lavender was the first thing that hit Daisy. That and the tall French window that reflected the evening light.

The wallpapers on the wall displayed beautiful flowers, and they added a bit of color to the otherwise neutral room.

There was a cream couch in the corner of the room, and a beige quilt was folded right on top of it.

The bed was a soft-looking thing with curtains hanging above it. Daisy resisted the urge to jump onto it.

"Your bathroom is right there. I'll leave you be. Please call me if you need anything. You can press that button if you need me. Dinner will be ready soon." Wanda pointed at a remote that was on the stool beside her bed.

"Thank you," Daisy said softly, still mesmerized by the beautiful room. Wanda bowed again before leaving her.

Daisy looked around the room and sighed. She was very tired and wished she could just lay down and fall asleep.

She quickly stripped and opened the bathroom. There was a Jacuzzi in the middle of the bathroom, and Daisy quickly figured out how to operate it.

She laid down and turned the water on. She sighed with relief as the jets of water massaged the knots in her body.

Reluctantly, she turned off the Jacuzzi and reached out for a towel but found nothing. Then she remembered there was a folded towel on her bed, which she had forgotten to take. She decided to do the quick walk naked to her bed and walked back into the room.

Daisy screamed when she saw Richard standing there. He immediately turned around, and his eyes widened when he took in the sight before him.

He turned his back immediately, and Daisy scrambled and grabbed a towel.

Richard spoke in a rush. "I'm sorry. I only came to drop the phone off. I'll leave now."

Daisy threw herself to the bed as tears brimmed in her eyes. Richard opened and closed his mouth but decided against saying anything and walked out of the room.

Daisy replayed walking out naked and wailed all over again. She cried herself to sleep.

Chapter 3

Daisy woke up with puffy eyes and matted hair, and her stomach rumbled, reminding her that she hadn't eaten at all since the previous night.

She pressed the button, and a few minutes later, Wanda appeared in the room.

"Good morning. If it's not a bother, I'd like to have some breakfast, please."

Wanda chuckled. "It's never a bother, ma'am. Moreover, I noticed you hadn't eaten last night, so breakfast is ready. I'll get it up for you."

Daisy let out a breath of relief. "Oh, thank you. That'll be great."

Wanda went and returned with a tray of different meals. Daisy's mouth watered at the sight of the meals. She was only glad that she could eat something.

That was when she noticed the flower and note on the tray. Daisy picked up the note, and it said, *I'm sorry about last night. Want to make it up to you. I'll see you by twelve.–R.*

Daisy scoffed. Why was Richard so sure she would say yes? Still, her curiosity got the better of her, and she wanted to see what he wanted to do.

Daisy lazed around for a bit before picking up her cell phone. She turned it on and went through the phone. She saw that she already had her mother's number saved. So Daisy assumed that they had got their mother a phone. She was also surprised to see her siblings' names, meaning they had also gotten cell phones.

She called Jack, and he picked it on the third ring. "Heyyy! Guys, it's Daisy." Soon enough, the voices of her other siblings rang through the phone.

She spoke to her siblings and laughed as they delightfully told her they would be going back to school soon.

Daisy still didn't want to speak to her mother and made no attempts to call her. She hung up and hugged the phone to her chest. At least she could call them until she decided to go and visit them.

Daisy showered and, this time made sure the door was locked, and she had a towel wrapped around her. She opened the wardrobe to reveal the gorgeous dress.

She settled for a short flowery dress with a high neckline. There was a shoe rack that had the perfect shoe for her feet, and she picked out a pair of flats.

Daisy stared at her curly hair and was glad to see the rows of hair products available. She rubbed in some moisturizer and used a curling iron to tame her hair.

Daisy didn't want to do too much, so all she did was rub a bit of lip-gloss and some mascara. It was enough for her.

She climbed down the stairs and saw that Richard had his back to her. He was standing in the living room with a phone to his ear.

He was dressed less formally than the first time they had met. He had a plain polo shirt with dark grey jeans, which he paired with sneakers.

He turned around and paused as he caught the sight of Daisy. He said something to his phone and hung up.

Daisy cleared her throat as he stared intently and descended the stairs.

"You look good," Richard said. He turned to walk out of the house, and Daisy followed.

"Thank you."

There was a sports car waiting in front of the house, and Richard opened the passenger door for her before getting into the driver seat himself.

"Where are we going?" Daisy asked as he revved out of the driveway.

"Just to give you a tour of the city. You might as well get used to your new location."

Daisy nodded and stared out the tinted window. Everyone around looked like they were going to a fashion show. It was modern, trendy and all too new to Daisy.

She hoped that it wouldn't be too difficult for her to adjust to her new surroundings.

Daisy gasped when she saw Richard's face on a large billboard. He had some suit on, and he was on a horse. The caption on the billboard read *Knight in shining armor: King of horseracing.*

"Wait, that's you." She pointed at the billboard.

Richard glanced at it and smiled. "Oh yeah, I guess so."

"You're a horse racer?"

Richard shrugged. "I prefer to call myself a cowboy, but same difference."

Daisy looked at him in a different light. She realized how it must have looked for him, getting into a fight with the kind of popularity he had, regardless of the intention.

Richard pulled up in front of an open space, and they got down from the car.

Richard led the way, occasionally glancing to see that Daisy was right behind him. She ignored the warm fuzzy feeling in her chest at the gesture and looked straight ahead.

A man came to meet them with a smile and introduced himself to Daisy. "Hello, I'm Phil. Please let me show you around."

Phil was a tiny round man that looked like he had all the contentment of the world.

He showed them the horses roaming on the field, and then they walked into a very large barn.

"Come, I'll show you my horses," Richard said. Daisy noticed that he seemed to be at peace, and they walked up to a stall.

Right in the stall, chewing a carrot was one of the most beautiful animals that Daisy had ever seen. It was a white horse with stripes of brown on the forehead.

Richard looked at the animal with softness. "This is Starr; I make use of her most of the time during my races. Don't worry; she's friendly."

Richard placed a cube of sugar in Daisy's hand. "Go on, feed her."

Daisy shook her head fearfully at the large horse. Richard chuckled and got behind her. He held her hand and stretched it towards Starr, who took the cube into her mouth and chewed the sugar.

Daisy was affected by her proximity and was terrified that her heart would jump out of her chest. He smelled like the forest after a rainy day, and she found herself breathing in his scent.

Richard turned to stare at her, and for a minute, time stood still between them. Daisy swallowed, and the spell was broken.

"Would you like to ride a horse, Ma?" The sound of Phil's voice startled Daisy as she had forgotten that he was with them.

"Yes, of course."

Richard introduced her to other horses, Lightening and Ginger, each of them living up to their names.

With the assurance of Phil, Daisy climbed into Ginger, and they rode in circles. Soon, Richard took over, and Phil left them to be.

"How long have you been racing?" Daisy asked as the horse slowly walked around.

"Hmm, since I was 14."

Daisy raised a brow. "And how old are you now?"

"Thirty-five."

Daisy was a bit surprised. She had assumed he was younger than that. He definitely looked younger than his age.

"I'll assume you like doing something?" Richard looked at her.

Daisy shrugged and fumbled with her dress. She hadn't told many people about her sewing, and the few people she had told treated it like it was just a hobby to pass the time, not something she was truly passionate about. "I guess I do like sewing."

"Really?"

"Yeah." Daisy found her tongue loosening. "I mean, I'll love to make something out of it. Maybe a sewing business or a fashion line, but I guess we can all dream."

Richard stopped in his steps. "It doesn't have to be a mere dream."

Daisy shook her head daintily. "Oh, it is. And that's okay. I've come to terms with it a long time ago."

Richard looked like he wanted to say more but decided against it.

They returned Ginger to the stall and waved goodbye at Phil.

"You didn't ride." Daisy pointed out as they drove out of the field.

Richard shrugged. "I prefer to ride hard, and since I'm on suspension, I can't do that."

"Right." Daisy felt disappointment in her heart. For a minute, she had forgotten all of this was just a show to make his suspension easier, and it wasn't real. She put on a shaky smile and looked out the window at a new world she had miraculously walked into.

They pulled up in a restaurant, and Daisy was taken aback by the restaurant's ambience. It was clearly an expensive one, and the fact that they took them to a private area confirmed that fact.

"What would you like to have?" Richard repeated the words that the waiter had said to Daisy.

"I'll get what you get."

Richard ordered some pasta with special sauce, and Daisy was glad he did.

She ate the delicious meal and savored the taste of the rich sauce against her tongue.

Daisy was surprised that she was comfortable with Richard's company. She also began to notice little things about him, like how he stuck his tongue out a bit when he was concentrating and how he nodded each time he zoned out.

Finally, they were full and decided to head back home.

Daisy was glad she had left the house, and she told Richard.

"My pleasure. Anything to make up for last night."

The car ride was more comfortable than before, and Daisy noticed that she wasn't sitting on the edge of her seat as she used to. A popular song played on the radio, and everything felt normal.

They pulled up at the house, and Daisy smiled at Fredrick, which was the butler's name, as he greeted them.

"Dinner is ready, sir." He said to Richard.

Richard waved him off as they walked into the house. "Oh, we already ate. Treat yourselves to the meals."

Daisy was touched by his generosity and clearly, so was Fredrick.

He turned to Daisy. "I have one last thing to show you. Come."

He grabbed her hand, and Daisy felt electricity run through her veins. She swallowed and hoped that he didn't notice it. They climbed up the stairs and turned into the corridor. Right at the end of the hallway was a door, and when Richard opened it, Daisy saw that it led to the rooftop.

She breathed in sharply at the view. It was evening, and the moon was only peeping out. They could see hundreds of buildings from where they were, and Daisy couldn't help but admire how beautiful the city was.

"It's beautiful." She said softly.

"Yeah, it is." She turned to see Richard staring at her as he spoke.

Daisy rubbed her hands as the cold air seeped through her clothes.

"Do you want to leave?"

Daisy shook her head. "No, I kind of want to admire the view for now."

"Then come here before you freeze." Richard pulled her closer and wrapped his arms around her. Daisy felt the chills disappear as his warmth seeped through her skin.

Together, they stared at the beautiful view and the beats of their hearts synced.

Daisy felt the electricity between them and could feel something stir in her chest.

Richard turned her around to look at her eyes as if he felt it too. "Can I kiss you? I think I might go crazy."

Daisy swallowed and nodded. Richard slowly leaned in and placed his lips on hers. He moved them in such a way that it felt like he was making love to her mouth.

Daisy gasped at the intense feeling of it all. She had only kissed a handful of men, and nothing felt as exhilarating as this.

She moaned as he deepened the kiss and pulled her closer. Daisy threw all caution to the wind and allowed him to wrap his arms around her.

There was a long bench screwed to the ground in the corner, and Richard sat on it with Daisy on his thighs. He kissed her deeply, and she felt her eyes roll to the back of her head as he reached for her breasts and fondled her nipples.

Daisy grinded against his groin and could feel the hard print of his member.

A bird cawed, and that was when Daisy snapped back to her senses. All the blood rushed to her face as she realized what she was doing.

She quickly scrambled from her seat and rushed away from the rooftop and down the hallway leading to her room.

She shut the door behind her and held a hand to her plump lips. What was she thinking?

Chapter 4

Daisy went all out to avoid Richard. Wanda nodded with understanding when she requested that all her meals be taken to the room. She couldn't imagine having to face him.

Alas, the day came when she had to see him. Owen had texted her, informing her of a fundraising she had to go to with Richard. They had to present themselves as a couple, and Daisy knew she had to fulfil that part of their contract.

An entire team of wardrobe assistants had helped her prepare for the event, and Daisy gasped as she looked at herself in the mirror.

She was wearing a dark blue knee-length dress with a one-hand sleeve. It made her skin tone pop out, and Daisy was amazed by what they had done to her hair. It had been curled into a side swoop, and she looked like royalty. They had paired the outfit with silver shoes and a silver purse.

Soon enough, Daisy knew she had to go downstairs, and she prepared herself mentally to see Richard.

She slowly descended the stairs, and Martha smiled at her with wonder. "Ma'am, you look amazing."

Richard turned as he heard Martha comment and froze in his steps when he saw Daisy. Daisy could also feel her heart thump as she took in the sight of him in his black tux.

His hair had been swept back with some hair product, making him look like James Bond but more handsome.

She let out a grave breath and said a silent prayer to be able to control herself.

"You look... good." Richard looked like he wanted to say more than that but decided against it.

Daisy nodded and whispered her thanks. They walked up to the Limousine, and Richard opened the door, ensuring that she entered first.

Daisy stole glances at him all through the car ride. He was unbelievable and some, and she wondered why he hadn't gotten a better person to be his fake fiancé. Why had it been her?

Richard simply used his phone all through, and Daisy swallowed her disappointment, paying attention to the music playing.

She had wished he'd, at the very least, act like something had happened between them. But he was as quiet as ever.

Thankfully, they pulled up at the location. It was a large state-of-the-art architectural building with people in formal clothes pooling in and out. There were cars all packed outside the building, and as Richard opened the door for Daisy to come down, she saw how all eyes turned on her.

She nervously adjusted her fur jacket, and Richard leaned in, whispering, "They've got nothing on you. Don't be worried."

Daisy nodded and exhaled. She held her head up high, and they walked right into the building.

Soft violin echoed through the large room, and Daisy could see waiters holding glasses of wine.

Owen spotted them and went over to meet them. He was wearing a tux similar to Richard's. He smiled at Daisy and kissed her hand. "You look lovely."

"Thank you, sir– Owen," Daisy remembered that he didn't like her calling him sir.

Owen and Richard chatted for a bit; then he let them be.

Daisy looked around and could see women whispering behind their hands as they assessed her. The stories of them had spread like wildfire, and it was time to be at the forefront of all that attention.

Richard held on to her hand, and Daisy drew comfort from that.

"Oh great, my ex is coming here," Richard murmured as a woman sashayed to them.

Her bold red lips curled into a smile when she saw Richard. She placed her hand on her curvy hips and stood in front of them.

"Richard. It's nice to see you again."

"Samantha. I wish I could say the same."

Richard grimaced.

Samantha laughed and waved it off. "Oh, come on, I thought you'd have gotten over that already."

Richard pulled Daisy closer. "As you can see, I have."

Samantha looked at Daisy and narrowed her eyes. She turned back to Richard. "You should come see me soon. I have a new apartment, and the bedroom is just amazing."

Daisy was stunned by the woman's boldness. She folded her arms and looked right into Samantha's eyes. "No, he can't, as you can see. He's with me."

Samantha scoffed and walked away.

"Well, well, that was something," Richard teased Daisy.

"I just couldn't stand her anymore."

"Sure." Richard kissed her on the cheek. She knew it was all for a show, but for that moment, Daisy pretended like all of it was real.

The party hostess was a popular actress and her business mogul husband. "And now, we'll have Mr. Richard Branson give us the opening speech."

Claps erupted in the room, and Richard squeezed her arm before walking up to the podium. She knew how easy it was for him to fit in. He walked with an air of grace and commanded everyone in the room to pay attention to him.

Richard waved a hand, and the claps slowly died out. "I'm grateful for this opportunity to be able to contribute positively to the lives of children. Education is an important aspect of life, and it's amazing that we are all making this a reality for children in this city."

Everyone clapped as he said this. Richard continued. "I met someone who told me that a dream was just a dream. That's not true. A dream can be a reality only if you want it to be."

Daisy inhaled as soon as she realized what he was talking about.

"And I want that person to pursue their dream, regardless of how hard it seems or how long it'll take. Never give up."

Everyone in the room cheered for Richard, and he climbed down the podium and made his way to Daisy.

She could feel the cameras around them capturing their moments, but she didn't really care. All she wanted was him by her side.

"Nice speech."

Richard smiled at her. "Well, I was hoping you'll like it."

They began to play ballroom music, and Richard held out a hand to Daisy. She accepted it, and he pulled her onto the dance floor.

They swayed to the music, and Daisy placed her head on his shoulder. She was still unsure about many things, but everything felt right at that moment.

A bell of alarm went off in her head when she realized what was really happening. She was falling for him. She was falling for the man she was betrothed to, and she didn't know if there was anything she could do about it.

"I have to go to the bathroom," Daisy said as she felt the pressure on her crotch.

"Okay. I'll be here."

Daisy nodded and made her way to the bathroom. She asked a waiter who quickly directed the way for her.

Daisy got to the bathroom and went into an open stall. She could see the women in the bathroom staring at her with recognition. She just wanted to do her business and leave.

Her phone chimed, and Daisy took a look at it. It was from Lisa, and she had sent the screenshot of a headline.

A modern-day Cinderella? Here's the tea on Richard Branson's new woman.

It was followed by a text. *Are you okay?*

Daisy quickly typed out a response. *I'm alright. Just make sure you don't get into any trouble and have fun at school. Also, tell the others I miss them.*

Will do. Bye.

Daisy put her phone back into her purse and came out of the cubicle. She quickly washed her hands and made her way out of the toilet.

Daisy went back to the hall but couldn't find Richard. She looked around yet she didn't see him.

She sent him a text, but he didn't respond. Daisy went outside just in case he was in the car for some reason.

She rounded the corner, and her heart fell when she saw what was happening right in front of her.

Richard and Samantha were kissing. It was dark, but she knew Richard anywhere, and she could recognize the glow from Samantha's dress.

Daisy choked and ran away from them. She rounded the corner and made her way to the waiting limousine.

"Please take me home," Daisy said as tears streamed down her face.

"Ma'am, are you–"

"Please just take me home."

The driver nodded and didn't say anything. He revved the car and drove out of the parking lot.

All Daisy could feel was her heart breaking into a million pieces.

Chapter 5

Daisy didn't bother talking to Richard. He spent most of the night knocking on her door, begging her to open the door, but she refused to. She didn't think she could handle seeing him.

Daisy made a call to Owen and told him she wanted to call the contract off. He tried to convince her, but she stood her ground. Her heart was too invested already.

She had only been there for over a month, but somehow, she felt hollow leaving new Orleans behind.

All through the flight back home, Daisy had tried to distract herself, but each time she shut her eyes, all she could see was Richard.

Finally, she got into Allendale, and while she was glad to see home, she also realized it was never going to be sufficient for her anymore.

She had seen the bigger city and wanted more of it.

Drew was the only one of her siblings at home, as the others were already in college. He hugged her tightly as soon as she opened the door to the house.

"Daisy! I didn't know you were coming." He had grown some inches taller, and Daisy ruffled his hair.

"Well, here I am."

"Daisy? Oh, it's you. Are you okay?" It was Martha. She wrung her hands with worry but was hesitant about approaching Daisy.

Daisy walked up to her and hugged her mother. She was tired of fighting and just wished to be comforted. Her throat seized up as tears filled her eyes.

"Oh, sweetheart. I'm here now." Martha patted her back and held her face. "You can stay here. I'm sorry I ever let you go in the first place."

Daisy sniffed. "It's okay. I'm here now."

Daisy ate some chicken soup before going back to her old room. Her mother had replaced the bunk with a single large bed, and Daisy fell onto it, drifting to sleep.

*****

Martha had been asking Daisy what had happened, but she didn't get any response from her, and Daisy told her not to contact Richard. It was good for her to let it go.

A week had passed, and she didn't feel her heart healing. If anything, she missed him even more. Richard had been texting and calling, but Daisy had ignored it all.

She spent all morning and night sewing, trying to distract herself.

Daisy was working on a piece of fabric when a text came in.

It was from an unknown number, and out of curiosity, she opened it.

Hey, I wasn't sure you'd talk to me if I called, so I decided to text. Honestly, I couldn't care less, but I feel I have to do this. I know you saw Richard and me that night, and I just want to tell you it's not what you think.

I was the one who kissed him, and if you had waited a little longer, you'd have seen him push me away. He's very fond of you, and you'll be stupid to let a man like that go. If I could, I'd steal him from you.

Samantha.

Daisy dropped her phone. She hung her head in her hands with regret. It was too late for anything. It didn't matter anyway; it was all over.

Martha popped her head into the room. "Hey, someone's here to see you."

"Who?"

"Um, I think you might want to see."

She lifted an eyebrow at her mother's odd behavior but decided to go downstairs. Martha hung back as Daisy opened the door.

Standing in front of her was Richard. His hair was unkempt, and he looked like he hadn't shaved for days.

"Hey," Richard said. His eyes looked tired as if he hadn't slept.

Daisy felt her heart explode in her chest. "Hey."

Not much was said, but enough had been spoken.

Drew was at school, so it was just Daisy and Martha at home.

Martha cleared her throat. "I have to be at the farmer's market; I'll see you in the evening. I'll leave you two to talk." She carried a basket and walked out of the house.

"Come in." Daisy ushered Richard in. As he walked past her, his hand grazed against hers, and she felt all the hair on her body stand.

He sat on the couch and looked at her warily. "I just want you to hear me out."

Daisy nodded.

"My mother died when I was fourteen, and she was my father's mistress. I blamed my father for her death because she died of loneliness. I hated that I was never enough for her, and she had to leave me here. I hit that man because he was mocking my mother, and I couldn't have it. But also because I had so much guilt in me.

"But when I met you, I didn't know what to expect. You were like a breath of fresh air for me, and I don't want to lose you. I don't know why you left suddenly, but I'm sorry. Whatever it is I've done, I'm sorry."

Daisy's heart broke for him, but she knew she had fallen in love with the man in front of her. "Oh, Richard." She moved closer to him and kissed him deeply.

Richard was surprised at first but responded with the same enthusiasm. Their bodies called out for each other, and soon enough, they made their way up to her bedroom.

Daisy wanted to give herself to him, and she allowed him to lay her onto the bed gently. He fondled her breast, and she moaned with desire. It was nothing like she had ever known.

Daisy pulled his shirt over his head and inhaled his familiar scent. She wanted them to be joined already and let him pull her underwear down.

Daisy kissed his body as he gently inserted a finger into her. Her body shook with ecstasy as she felt it was too much to handle.

"Can I?" Richard whispered into her ears.

Daisy nodded and spread her legs apart for him, ready to be consumed by him.

Richard slowly inserted his member into her, and together, they rode on the waves of exhilaration.

They both panted as soon as they had calmed down, and Richard wrapped his arms around her.

"Can we start again?"

Daisy looked into his grey eyes and nodded. "Yes."

"Okay. Hi, I'm Richard Owen, and I think you are the most beautiful girl I ever met."

Daisy giggled. "Hi, I'm Daisy Hatfield, and I think you are the most attractive man I ever met."

Richard kissed her forehead, and they embraced each other.

Daisy's phone rang, and she picked up the call.

"Hello?"

"Hello. Am I speaking to Daisy Hatfield, please?"

"Yes, you are. Who's this?"

"Oh, great. This is to inform you that you have been accepted to be a student in Oakland Fashion school, New

Orleans for this fall. I'll be forwarding more information to you after this phone call."

Daisy blinked. She couldn't believe what she was hearing. "Oh my God, thank you. Thank you."

She hung up and told Richard the news.

He gave her a genuine smile. "See, dreams can be realities."

"Yes. Oh my gosh, yes."

"Now, Daisy Hatfield, will you be mine? Stay with me?"

At that moment, Daisy wanted nothing more. "Yes, yes, I'll be yours. Forever."

THE END

Winning Him Over

Description

Barb is a twenty-four year old young woman who graduated from City University in her hometown about two years agao. She was an average student but it didn't bother her because she had felt that her physical assets would ultimately determine her fate.

Barb is a a big beautiful woman and any man would want to have her to himself. Owing to her attractiveness, she works steadily as a plus size model as well as being the weekend anchor on the local television station.

She had just won first place in the Miss Beautiful pageant when a man approached her. He had a purely masculine and handsome features. He was definitely striking, possessing an obvious confidence. Locking eyes, Barb noticed a sly grin upon his face and a twinkle in his. Now Barb wished more than anything she could be with him.

Chapter 1

My name is Barb Wilder. I am twenty-fours years old, and graduated two years ago from City University. I wasn't the best student. However, I felt that my physical assets would ultimately determine my fate. My family, consisting of my parents, both high-level executives for large multinational firms, and my older brother, a doctor in residence, didn't quite understand me. Yet, they didn't really nag me about academics either. I won't try to be modest in describing my body. I am a big beautiful woman, and any man would want to have me to himself. My jet-black hair extends to the middle of my back. My skin is flawlessly light-colored. Owing to my attractiveness, I work steadily as a plus size model. On the weekends, I do the news reporting on the local channel.

I had just won first place in the Miss Big and Beautiful pageant. I wasn't particularly surprised, figuring that the scores of the talent portion of the competition, in which I sang, would be heavily influenced by the impressions made by the earlier swimsuit part of the contest. Still, it was a thrill when I was announced as the winner, especially since it was over my long-time frenemy, Nan, who placed second. Nan is, I have to admit, twice as good a singer as I. However, most would consider me more physically captivating. We had been holding hands as the two finalists. When my name was announced as the winner, Nan, during the obligatory fake-hugging immediately after the announcement, had whispered in my ear, "Congratulations on your victory, Barb, but this will be the last time that you beat me in anything." She then winked at me and I couldn't tell if she was being serious or not.

While the band was still playing, a man approached me. He had a masculine handsomeness. He was wearing a fine tuxedo, which could not hide his broad shoulders and obviously muscular build. He wasn't particularly tall, being level with my height in my four-inch stiletto heels. But he was definitely striking, possessing an obvious confidence, and his eyes locked onto mine unwaveringly, a hint of a smile gracing his visage. As he drew nearer, I saw a badge that indicated that he had been one of the judges of the pageant.

"Miss Wilder, you are one very impressive woman, the whole package. I want to introduce myself. Louis Smith. I always stay tuned to the television whenever you're on and have been interested in meeting you for some time now."

"The pleasure is all mine, Mr. Smith. Please call me Barb," I purred, as I extended my hand. Louis took my hand and gave it a soft kiss. Of course, like most trendy city residents, I was familiar with the name, if not exactly the face. The gossip papers and websites had all declared him one of the regions top ten eligible bachelors ever since he returned back from Europe about eight months ago. His family was among the wealthiest in the city, with countless holdings in commercial and residential properties. He is a billionaire himself aside from his family's wealthiness. Louis, twenty-oneyears of age, had been sent six years ago in London to acquire an MBA and to cut his managerial chops by overseeing family properties in Europe. In his spare time over there, Louis co-founded an Internet start-up, which had been bought by another start-up for a hefty profit. The family had apparently called Louis back to work full-time to help manage their more extensive North American assets. The Smiths were an old-school family, very private. Even in the gossip rags, there were very few details about him and even fewer photographs of Louis' activities around the city.

"Do you know what impressed me the most about you, Barb?"

"Was it my precise pitch on the high notes?" I joked.

"Well, those were quite lovely," he chuckled. "However, I am truly impressed by your natural elegance and your big beautiful body. You exude such confidence in various situations and you carry yourself with unbelievably regal sophistication."

"Thank you, Mr. Smith. I'll still on a high from winning, so keep my high going by complimenting me more," I laughed.

"Barb, on stage there, you were a woman among girls. I would love to throw more compliments at you at a later time. Would you do me the pleasure of giving me your number? Perhaps we could have a date soon." Louis Smith then tilted his head, locked deeply into my eyes and smiled broadly, almost challenging me to try to deny his request.

"It would be my pleasure, Mr. Smith. A woman can never listen to enough compliments, especially from someone so handsome." I winked at him and then recited my number into his phone.

"Excellent, Barb! I look forward to meeting again." He headed stage right. I was then mobbed by a number of pageant officials.

As Louis Smith was about to disappear from view, I noticed that Nan had intercepted him. She was speaking to him alone. I could see her whispering into his ear at times and giggling often and playfully touching him frequently, while he seemed to have no interest in ending their conversation. After about ten minutes, however, they did go their separate ways, but not before I saw her speak into her phone.

Two hours later, after the obligatory pictures had been taken and the forms had all been signed and upcoming post-pageant meetings had been scheduled, I had finished changing into my street clothes. I was waiting for my family to take me to a small private celebration party in their apartment, when my phone rang. It was Louis Smith. "I was interested in setting up our date, Barb. Would you be free this weekend?"

I already had plans all next weekend to be away to visit with friends and attend a bachelorette party. Still, I was determined that it probably would not be wise to be unavailable for Louis Smith. I reasoned that he probably had other appealing women immediately available to him and playing hard-to-get could possibly result in never getting together. More concerning, though, was Nan's flagrant attempt at seducing him earlier and I wanted to make sure that I got to him first.

"You flatter me with your strong interest, Mr. Smith. I do have some free time this weekend. When were you thinking of?"

"All weekend, Barb. You would need to let the television station know that you will be occupied. I would like to get to know you deeply ... intimately, you might say. I've found that doing so requires an extended and concentrated amount of time together. I am quite busy and I'm used to making important decisions over short periods of time. This includes my choice of companions. I would ask that you clear your schedule from Friday evening to Monday morning. The date will continue, as long as we are getting along well. If one of us decides to terminate our date earlier in the weekend, well, I think we could both maturely go our separate ways. I see this as the best way to start learning about each other, don't you think, Barb?"

"Um, yes, you're kind of convincing, Mr. Smith. I guess I can re-arrange my schedule for you ...I mean, us."

"Call me Louis, Barb. And I understand that you may have plans already. A stunning woman like you rarely just sits at home. So, I'm offering you this. Call me on Tuesday. Tell me what you would like to do Friday evening, Saturday afternoon, Saturday evening, and Sunday afternoon. I'll make it happen. Deal?"

"Absolutely, a deal. I'm looking forward to learning about ... us, Louis."

"Great! Oh, by the way, if you wish to purchase anything for our weekend together, call my personal assistant, Jen. I'll text you her number. She can pay for many things that you may desire. In fact, I insist that you avail yourself of this offer. I'm taking up your time at the last minute and I would like to repay you in some trivial way for it. Also, if you have any requests, please convey them to her and she will see what she can do. I have to go now. Bye-bye, Barb."

"Bye, Louis. See you on Friday." The phone connection ended.

I thought about things the next day. It was quite clear that I would be expected to have a sexual relationship with Louis on Friday evening. It wasn't exactly what I wanted, as I have only had sex on a first date only once previously and it was not a particularly fond. On the other hand, I decided that I really did want to pursue this billionaire and charismatic man. If that was what he expected and the arrangement of an entire weekend date would imply this, then I determined that denying him would not further my goals. He would probably terminate the date early and would find ways to relieve his frustrations without me. So, my strategy for the weekend was to have sex early and often, but otherwise keeping him interested by being compelling in other ways—good conversation, being adventurous, demonstrating non-sexual talents. I found it weird that key elements of our rendezvous were quite unconventional. The man had proposed a first date, but I was the one scheduling activities and sexual intercourse was already presumed.

I called Jen on Monday. "Yes, Miss Wilder. Mr. Smith told me you might call," she said, after I had introduced myself. "How may I help you?"

"Louis mentioned that if I wanted to purchase some items, that I should call you. Is that right? If so, I may be buying some clothes and accessories. Would that be too presumptuous?"

She replied curtly, "No, of course not. Mr. Smith is very generous with money, but he does have high standards, so do go for quality, Ms. Wilder. That is my advice to you. I figure that if you keep the costs under seventy-five thousand dollars, that would be absolutely fine. By the way, don't buy any jewelry. Two reasons, the first is that every item bought will technically be his, so you can't presume to keep any jewelry. Second, he will probably buy you a necklace anyway this weekend. Anything else, Ms. Wilder?"

"Oh yes. I would like to see if I could come over to Louis' residence Friday morning. I decided that for Friday evening, we could just have a private dinner at his place. I wanted to prepare myself for the evening over there."

"I would need to check with Mr. Smith, but I suspect that would be fine. I'll let you know the next time you call and I helping you finalize purchases."

I got to work. I had only a couple of short photo shoots and a few meals with my family and friends scheduled for the week. So I had plenty of time to plan for what I considered to be a very important weekend.

After working out at the gym and getting a French manicure, I arrived mid-morning at Louis' lavish four-bedroom penthouse in the Golden Mile district. Jen met me at the door. I was slightly surprised by her appearance, as I had expected someone much older. Jen seemed to be roughly my age and was quite attractive in her white short pencil-skirt suit with matching high-heeled pumps; I wondered if there was a backstory to her employment with Louis. She showed me into a large guestroom with its own bathroom. After a very business-like tour of the penthouse, Jen left. I unpacked my clothes and placed them inside the walk-in closet and took a bath.

At noon, a chef arrived, also young and remarkably attractive, although her figure was largely hidden by her frumpy work attire. She introduced herself as Carina and made me a noodle dish for lunch. She then began preparing a dinner for two. While she was making dinner, the hairstylist from the studio came up, a personal favor to me. He gaped at the opulence of the apartment and told me that it would seem that he would have to do some of his most fabulous work with me today. He did, leaving me with a magnificent, voluminous updo that left my neck tastefully bare and a few tendrils of hair framing my face. The look appeared both innocent and sophisticated. Both my hairstylist and the cook left mid-afternoon, which left me with a few hours before Louis would come back.

I started by having a clean shave to make my skin feel sexy smooth. I did leave a small rectangular landing strip around my vagina. I figured that I could invite Louis to remove that later, if he so wanted. I spent over an hour doing my eyes, just to ensure that my lashes were thick and long, my brows were shaped and penciled flawlessly, and that the light bronze eye shadow with just a touch of shimmer gave off the right look. I applied a hint of pink blush to highlight my cheekbones. I sprayed perfume on my neck, wrists, breast cleavage, and inner thighs.

Then I dressed. I had spent only half of the budget limit on my outfits for the days with Louis and I was certain that it would pay off. I slipped on a black thong which barely covered my landing strip. It certainlycouldn't quite cover my puffy pussy lips, and turned into floss on the backside. It wasn't really serving any real functional purpose, but I knew that either Louis or I could have fun with it. My little black dress was a clingy silk cowled halter. The cowl plunged past my chest and was adorned at its bottom near my navel with a diamond-jeweled medallion. The inner halves of my large and firm breasts were fully displayed.

The cut of the dress left the side of my breasts visible and my entire back naked down to the crack of my ass. The design of the dress did not permit a bra, thus the points of my nipples were vaguely visible through the fabric. The hem, being six inches above the knee, gave the illusion of being slightly more conservative, but there was a long slit along the right side that ended level with my "kitty." I had bought a befitting size model, smaller than my usual size, so the dress was skin tight, with the result that a deep cleavage was created and that my ass and thighs appeared to be simply painted black.

Even so, I had selected the dress well. It was obviously well-cut and designed, showing sophistication and quality, so that the initial impression would be elegance rather than slutty.

I fastened on my shoes. They were black Manolo Blahnik sandals with two-inch platforms, each with a single half-inch front strap that ran across the slightly behind the toes and a buckled criss-crossing ankle strap around the back. Each sandal had a six-inch gold metallic stiletto heel and my slender and shapely legs looked fantastic with that elevation. I had carefully chosen the dimensions of my footwear. Wearing these shoes would leave probably leave me a few inches taller than Louis in his bare feet, but lengthening the appearance of my legs was just the impression I wanted. And like my dress, the shoes were a size too small and left the tips of my toes just slightly overhanging the platform, which previous lovers had found to be advantageous when sucking on my toes. These sandals were clearly FMS, fuck-me shoes, although I didn't need the shoes to declare my intent, considering the design of my LBD.

I heard the front door open. Louis' voice shouted, "Barb, are you here? I'm back a little early. Couldn't wait to see you.

But finish up what you are doing. I'll get us a couple of drinks. Meet me in the living room."

"What a pleasant surprise to have you back so early, Louis. I'll just be another fifteen minutes. It'll be worth the slight wait, though," I replied loudly from the guestroom. I put on two-inch gold hoop earrings and a thin jade bracelet onto my left wrist. Jen had hinted that Louis might present me with a necklace, so I didn't wear one of my own. I looked at myself in a full-length mirror, giggling like a schoolgirl. I had achieved the exact effect I wanted. Angel from the neck up, devil from the neck down. Louis would be torn between trying to protect my innocence or trying to ravage my sinful body. Of course, the latter would win out, as it always does. I debated for a while and decided to tip the scales a bit more. I penciled around my naturally full lips, slightly puckered on the top and engorged on the bottom, ones that countless people assume are injected with collagen.

Then I applied bright red glossy lipstick over them, a clear invitation to intimacy, as if more hints were actually needed. Then I walked out of the guestroom.

Chapter 2

"Having you here, Barb, already makes it a great weekend." My arms were still wrapped around his neck, so Louis spoke with his lips just a few inches from mine.

"You promised me compliments for this date, cutie. Would you like to be more specific? Is it the possibility of listening to some of my great jokes? Or maybe my potential to advise you on some important business decisions?" I teased. Locking in on his eyes, I grazed his cock with the back of my right hand. I softly and suggestively said, "Would you like me to take a wild guess? Does it have anything to do with realizing what kind of fun you'll have eyeing me and playing with me for the next few days?"

Louis spoke in a controlled voice, at least initially. "Well, you are very mesmerizing, Barb. You are gorgeous and have a spectacular body. And you obviously spent significant time preparing yourself. Your make-up and hair, your flawless skin, your attire, so elegantly sensual. I'm not sure what I should do, maybe you could advise me. I want to take things slowly right now, to get to know the person behind that sweet innocent face.

"Such graceful lines, soulful eyes, cute nose, full lips. But I can't help myself, I am so drawn to you sexually. But your figure, your body, those huge breasts, that round ass, those long-toned legs, you have such a fuckable body, excuse my language ... ", he babbled, his words finally betraying his initial attempt at reigning in his libido.

"Do go on. I love that language," I whispered seductively.

"... I don't know whether to lose myself in a long kiss with you or to fuck ... fuck you raw." He panted the last phrase out.

"Maybe both, dear. But let's start with a kiss and see where that takes us. Oh, and please remember that this is the only outfit I have for dinner tonight, cutie," I said with deliberately confounding cheeriness. I tilted his head slightly and planted my lips directly on his, giving him a little peck.

His response was ravenous. He urgently engaged my lips and left them there. His hands wrapped around my backside and they began to determinedly explore and massage my back and butt. I felt his tongue lightly touching mine and I returned more firmly in kind. He then began exploring my mouth and I his. After about ten minutes of this, all in silence, Louis pulled from the kissing, but kept his hands around my ass. He lustily stared at my eyes for a good minute, as if trying to make up his mind about something.

He then dragged me down onto the plush carpet, in between the sofa and a large low-lying glass table, hands still on my ass, with him on the bottom. Then he resumed exploring my mouth with his tongue and massaging my back and ass with one hand and steadying my head with the other, all-in silence. After about five minutes, he again stopped and wordlessly stared into my eyes. For fun, I gave him my patented pouty cute look.

"Don't give me that, you slut," he muttered. He rolled me over. He unhurriedly and gently kissed my neck and I arched it high for him. He must have pecked at my neck at least twenty times, but the last one was a fiercely focused one that would certainly leave a hickey later. His entire body descended lower and lower, hands along my sides and legs, tenderly kissing his way down. My pussy, already moist from earlier, began to leak in response to his persistent oral attention to my body. I moved my right arm from the floor, placed it through the side slit of the skirt, and onto my clit.

Then I felt my breasts being kissed and licked, slowly and softly, one then the other, with agonizing patience, but without ever getting to my covered nipples. I might have climaxed right then, had he decided to suck on them. But he didn't, despite having his lips on my breasts for over five minutes. I couldn't take it anymore and wildly rubbed my clit with one hand and pressed on my mound with the other, desperately trying to achieve orgasm, as more juices leaked and soaked my sorry excuse for knickers. Then he surprised me by leaving my breasts, continuing to kiss down my belly until finally circling his tongue endlessly around my navel. As I continued to teeter at the edge, he whispered, "Clever girl, exposing so much skin in the front. I love tasting you, Barb. Now, can I help you down there?" I just moaned, breathing shallowly and rapidly.

He placed two fingers inside me. After just two strokes into my pussy, I convulsed violently and screamed, "FUUUUUCK MEEEEEE!" I began repeating, "Oh my God, Oh my God, Oh my God ...", as he metronomically went in and out at a sluggish pace. My whole body writhed and both hands gripped his shoulders in an attempt to get him to stop, the sensation becoming too intense. But he just steadily kept on stroking inside, while now using his other hand to furiously rub my clit, until I finally went limp and changed my orgasmic Whimpering, I said, "Please stop, please stop. I'll do anything for you, if you stop."

He stopped. After a bit, he growled menacingly, "Just what I was waiting to hear, my whore. Get on your knees." I slowly managed to get on all fours. He sat down on the couch. He resumed, flatly stating, "You know what to do."

I took my time unzipping his fly. By now, my head had cleared. He had no underwear on. I pulled out his circumcised cock, which was mostly hard. I was not particularly skilled with fellatio, having not had much practice until only more recently; fellatio is fundamentally a submissive act and I was used to the majority of my previous lovers trying to please me than the other way around. Still, I knew the basics. I made sure he saw me lick my lips and kiss the tip of his cock a number of times, all while gazing at him submissively. I languidly circled the head over and over, eyes still in upgaze, pausing to lick the frenulum and the meatus each time. With each lick, I noticed Louis shuddered a bit. His cock was fully rigid now, a penis I estimated at about six inches and a bit more than an inch in diameter. I was glad at its normal dimensions, as I had never noticed a correlation between size and my personal pleasure and I hated the potential prospect of deep-throating something too big.

I broke off my gaze and concentrated on his member. Moving my head back and forth, I progressively enveloped the first three inches of his cock. My right hand jerked off the back half, with the long-manicured nails of my left-hand tickling underneath his scrotum. I made some non-specific cooing noises while slurping him. Louis wordlessly scanned what he could see of my body, certainly admiring my delicate neck, my toned back, my well-defined calves. At some point, I got the sense he was willing himself to ejaculate. "Keep it up, Barb. This blowjob feels so good. I wish this could go on forever. You are so talented. You have such a talented mouth. What a talented cock-sucker." He continued with variations of these phrases, all while closing his eyes.

I suspected that he was only rambling in order to drive himself to orgasm. Sure enough, within a minute, his penis jerked and I felt a small spurt in my mouth. I instantly pulled out and rapidly pumped his manhood with my hand, most of his cum landing on my neck and my chest, some of it staining the cowl of my dress. Even when he ran dry, I continued to pump, until finally his cock began to go flaccid.

I got up and cleaned both of us up with some tissue found on the glass table behind me. Louis simply stayed seated, eyes closed, with his head extended backward against the top of the sofa. When he finally opened his eyes to look at me, I mouthed, "Thank you."

He nodded. "No, thank YOU. You are so sexy, Barb. Your lips are so amazing around my mouth and around my cock. So incredibly full and so sensual."

"You are so kind. They are quite inviting, aren't they?" I agreed, puckering them a few times. My eyes twinkled as I continued, "Oops, you didn't mean down there, did you?"

Louis laughed. "I don't know yet. Maybe I'll get to find out later." He paused and looked at me yearningly. "I can't get over how responsive your body is, Barb. I can only imagine how it will react when we are nude together, making love tonight."

"Don't get ahead of yourself, sweetie. I am a conservative girl. What makes you think that'll happen?" I teased, a big smirk on my face.

"Because I'm going to treat you like a princess for the rest of the evening. You won't be able to resist my charms and you'll beg me to sleep with you tonight," he said with a touch of arrogance.

I decided to have fun with him. "The way I see it, dear, you won't be able to resist my sexy body, which I'll flaunt all evening until YOU beg to ravage me tonight."

Louis stood up, picked up two filled stemmed glasses from the center of the table and handed me one. "This champagne is probably flat by now. I poured it over an hour ago. Still, let's toast. To Barb, best wishes for winning her challenge."

"And to Louis," I followed. "Best wishes for winning his challenge." We intertwined our right arms and drained the flat champagne. I gave him a peck on his mouth. "Thank you for inviting me for the weekend. You're right, it will be a great weekend."

"You're welcome, Barb. The pleasure is all mine. Foreplay is now over, though. Time for the main course."

"What?" I exclaimed. "We each just had an orgasm. You have stamina for more?"

"I have stamina like you wouldn't believe, Miss Wilder. But, silly you. Did you think I meant another round of sex? All this physical activity has made me hungry and I believe Carina made us a delicious three-course meal." He extended his hand.

I could only laugh, as I took his hand and walked to the dining room.

It was a fine dinner. The nighttime view of city from his penthouse was magnificent. As were the food and the conversation, both enhanced by a bottle of vintage white wine that Louis told me he had had from before he left for London and was saving for a special occasion. He was a perfect gentleman, seated across from me in the middle of a long glass table meant for six. He listened attentively to what I had to say and was forthcoming with his own thoughts. For the most part, he focused on my eyes during our almost non-stop conversation, occasionally touching my arms or hands, generally undistracted my subtle and unsubtle attempts to display various features of my body.

Subtle, like often leaning my chest forward and frequently adjusting the halter straps around my chest. Unsubtle, like when I unbuckled my right stilletos, exposed my entire toned thigh through the slit of my dress, and slid my foot up his pant leg. I got the reaction I wanted for that trick, as Louis simply stared wide-eyed through the table and re-adjusted his pants to accommodate a growing bulge in his crotch. When he finally looked up, I simply winked at him and licked my lips with a grin.

Chapter 3

Despite my little teases, we did learn about each other. Louis told me stories about his activities in Britain and all over Europe. He told me that it was actually his idea to go there, finally convincing his family when he when he was accepted to university, and after he promised to manage and help grow the various family holdings in London and across Europe while there. He described how he and two friends from school worked long hours developing a real-estate website, building a real-world infrastructure around it, marketing it, watching it modestly take off, and finally negotiating a lucrative buyout. "That was the best thing I have ever done, Barb, not just the sale, but the process. I did it myself, minimal help from my family. Although, let's face it, not to take too much credit, I never had to worry about running out of funds for myself and some aspects were easier because of family connections and intuition honed by being around the family business. But what can I do, Barb, I am a child of my circumstances and I can't just pretend it doesn't exist, you know?"

"There must have been a lot of personal adjustments you had to make coming back here."

"A few. I'm a bit less dependent on help. I drive my own car. I do have people on my payroll, though, like my cook and my maid, both great finds. You probably already met my cook Carina, who is really talented at nourishing me, I think. She comes about three times a week. You won't be meeting my housekeeper Irene, though. She works here every day quietly before the sun even rises and many mid-afternoons when I'm at work. Mostly I see her when I can't sleep."

"Your assistant appears quite professional, too. I've had a number of conversations with her this week and met her earlier today."

Louis chuckled. "Jen. Jen is quite a revelation. My life would be significantly more frustrating without her. She is quite discreet and expertly satisfies all the crazy desires that I request of her." Louis then paused, ruminating over what he just said. "Just so you know, there's nothing personal between us, though. She is a complete professional, as you just noted, Barb."

I revealed to Louis I wanted to work more in the television or movie industry, not necessarily as an actress, but more on the production side. I wanted to be part of the creative process, both artistic and business, that existed on the other side of the camera. And I confided that I wanted to still be important when my beauty eventually faded. I didn't know whether he believed me or not. I'm not sure I would believe it, if someone like me said that. But it's the truth and t's the reason I regret the way I passed through higher education. I told him I entered the Miss Big and Beautiful pageant because I was hoping it could be my passport to the industry, obviously as an actress, even though I doubted I had acting talent and had only rudimentary training. I aspired to one day parlay acting gigs into writing or directing or producing. "I really pray that I get the chance one day to show the people who makes the shows that I am more than a pretty face ... and a body that powerful men would beg on their knees to fuck, of course." I added the last phrase with a grin. "Speaking of fuck, Louis, something just occurred to me."

"What would that be?"

"You know how you said you didn't know whether to lose yourself in a kiss with me or fuck me raw? You pretty much only did the first one."

"I know. It was what I felt most strongly at the time and I think it was the right choice. Don't you agree?"

"Don't you think you deserve more, sweetie?"

"Barb, don't trick me to win a bet," he replied, with a hearty laugh. "By the way, it's now ten o'clock. Do you still want to go out dancing?"

"Absolutely. I want to show off my killer moves for you, dear."

"Great! Do you think you can get ready in ten minutes? My housekeeper will clean all this up. Oh, and please just wear what you have on now, Barb, if that would be acceptable to you. I love your look. You have such great taste. By the way, what is your neck size?"

I told him and we walked to our separate rooms. I touched up my make-up, brushed my teeth and rinsed my mouth, and spritzed a touch more perfume. I went to the front door, waiting. Louis, now dressed in a stylish double-breasted dark suit, came out with a small box. He opened it, revealing a silver choker with a single row of diamonds.

"Thank you for clearing your schedule for me, Barb. Do you like it?"

"I love it, Louis!" I squealed.

"I bought three of the same style actually since I didn't know your size. My assistant will return the other two on Monday. May I put in on?"

"Of course. Don't let me distract you." I came in closer, pressing against his body, and kissed him on the right cheek, leaving a bright red impression on his face. Then I did the same to his right shirt collar, which also exposed the back of my neck. Louis took this opportunity to fasten the choker.

"Shall we?" Louis held my hand, as we walked out the door.

As we waited for the elevator, I said to him, "Just a warning. Don't wash off the lipstick from your face or your shirt until we get back. I want everyone to know you are mine, you are MY property. It's only fair anyway, with that big hickey you left on my neck from before dinner." He squeezed my hand lovingly, but did not actually look that amused.

I was told the dance club was about fifteen minutes away in the nighttime traffic. Louis drove a black Ferrari convertible and decided to leave the top open. It was hard to talk. So I took the opportunity to wet his appetite. I softly massaged his left thigh, ever so close to his obviously rigid cock, for much of the trip. I pulled out lipstick from my small clutch twice, so he could watch me apply it from the corner of his eye. At one point, without him noticing, I untied and tied back my halter, slipping the trailing part of the seat belt underneath it. And I exposed all of my right leg the entire ride. I made sure he noticed me deliberately admiring it and continuously running my hand across its length. When the club came into view, I asked him to stop.

"What's wrong?" he asked, pulling over.

"My panties are bothering me. They were soaked with my juices before dinner and they never dried out because my pussy has been constantly wet ever since." This last part was not really true, but what's wrong a little white lie anyway? "I need to take it off." I then slowly wiggled off the the damp piece of floss. "Just as I thought, quite moist. Would you be a dear and hold them for me in your coat?" I paused to sniff it before handing them over to Louis.

Louis shook his head, grinned, and put them in his breast pocket, as if it were a pocket square. He then drove over to the valet. I stayed in my seat, even after an attendant opened my door. Louis came over to my side, tipped the passenger side valet, and indicated he would take over. "Sweetie, I seem to have a problem here. Somehow the seat belt has tangled with my dress. Could you help me out?"

Louis looked closely and laughed. "Naughty girl," he said. "May I?" He began to pull the halter knot.

"Be careful. You wouldn't want my girls to pop out now, would you? God knows they want to, with them being so big and this dress being so confining," I said playfully.

"I'll take care to defend your honor, Barb ... at least for right now."

He untangled me. I then swung my legs out, making sure both were exposed up to the upper thighs. I slowly placed my right, then my left, fuck-me shoes on the ground, making sure Louis got a extended eyeful. I do have attractive legs. They are long and smooth, none of which I take particular credit for. They are also very toned and shapely, which I do take credit for, a product of extensive work at the gym; like most of my body, there is just enough fat to smooth out excessive muscle definition, but when I flex, the individual muscle groups come nicely into view. I winked at him before finally taking his hand to emerge from the deep bucket seat of the car.

We evidently had an approved reservation. After Louis talked to the doorman, we were brought through the front door by a host, cutting in front of a line that stretched half a block, populated with many women in tight skirts barely covering their ass. The host led us to the back and seated us at a dimly lighted private booth for two with a heavy wrap-around curtain. The club itself was full but not packed, with about a couple arms-length distance between guests. The centrally-located dance floor was slightly more packed. Moderately loud house music seemed to be the dominant musical style and conversing would require either a very loud voice or close proximity. A hostess came over shortly with two stem glasses and opened bottle of Dom Perignon for us. Louis and I downed a glass before I grabbed his hand and I whispered in his ear, "Come with me."

I am a fantastic dancer. I have taken lessons since youth for all types of dance and I have spent too many nights in dance clubs for me not to be in total control on the floor. Louis was both capable enough to keep up and savvy enough to just let me do my thing. For my part, when not touching him, I made sure to constantly maintain frequent eye and bodily contact. I occasionally held both his hands to pull him near me, while I writhed. And, of course, I frequently turned my back to him to grind my ass on his bulging crotch, while directing his hands to wrap around my pelvic region.

We returned back to our seats after about twenty minutes of this, just before developing any sweat. We people-watched for quite a while, having fun pointing out things to each other, laughing at some of the bad dancing and aborted pick-up attempts.

Eventually, Louis draped his left arm over my shoulder and I nestled my head on his chest, my right arm wrapped around his back and my left hand absent-mindedly groping between his legs. We sat silently, uninterested in speaking, secure in the current state of our relationship. After a while, I closed the curtain around our booth. In the privacy of our little world, I sat on his lap sideways and we began to kiss deeply, my hands on his head and his around my torso. I became increasingly excited and my bare pussy was starting to leak. Our lips still locked, I pushed him back onto the seat, so that he was underneath me. Louis was initially motionless, while I rapidly drove my hips up and down onto his crotch, trying to relieve my tension. I began to moan with greater desperation and Louis started to buck his hips a bit. "Help me, help me ... " I mouthed repeatedly.

Then, all of a sudden, my left arm hit the champagne bottle and it shattered on the floor, the sound loudly piercing through the music. The moment was ruined. I sat up and straightened up my dress. "I got a little carried away, sweetie. Sorry."

Attendants opened the curtain and fussed over us, trying to remove the glass and mop up the liquid. People were staring at us and the commotion around us. I decided to use the time to continue placing my lips all over Louis' face, marking my man for all to see. Louis, however, did not reciprocate my attention to him. Instead, he sat rather stiffly and tried to distance himself a bit. Sensing his unease, I stopped kissing him and apologized.

"Barb, nothing to be sorry about. Maybe we should leave, though. It's not a particularly private place here, anyway." I found it difficult, given my confidence in my ability to inspire lust in men, to believe that his interest in me was waning this early.

Perhaps, he was playing the game that lovers play when they are unsure of the other's true feelings, a defense mechanism. Taking it slow to make sure your interest will not be unrequited. I didn't know him well enough to know for sure what he was thinking, though. All I knew was that I was feeling possessive right now. I wanted his body and soul committed to me right now and I wanted to show it.

"I agree, cutie. Let's go back to your place. Maybe we can have fun there. Shall we use facilities before we leave?"

We both left our seats. I took longer in the bathroom, of course. When I emerged, I could see that Louis had already returned to the booth. I decided to make him a touch jealous in the remaining time left in the club. Trolling, I call it. Far from the booth, but clearly in Louis' line of sight, I pretended to be lost, standing alone. As expected, when a pretty woman with tits the size of grapefruits, a bubble-butt ass, slender legs that appear to stretch forever, and dressed to show off all of those assets stands alone by herself, a phenomenon like air rushing into a vacuum occurs. A tall and handsome man approached me, complimenting me on my general beauty and, oh, could he buy me a drink or would I like to dance? I flirted with him for a minute, adjusting my dress, telling him how attractive he was, laughing a bit, touching his forearm, and finally lied to him that I was with friends.

He offered his card and I placed it in my clutch. I walked somewhere else and, of course, a similar encounter repeated itself. After four of these encounters, I quit trolling and walked back to the booth.

Louis appeared a bit annoyed. "Ready to go?" he asked a bit brusquely.

"Sure, dear," I replied cheerfully, although I was actually a bit worried about how Louis perceived my little adventure just now.

We rode back in silence, even though the top of the convertible was now closed because of the coolness of the midnight air. I spent the drive massaging his neck, while he left both hands on the steering wheel. After parking the car, we went up the elevator, and entered his flat. Louis escorted me to my guestroom and turned on the lights for me. "It's been a long night, Barb. Thank you for the evening. I believe we still have some nice activities tomorrow, right?" he said in a subdued voice.

"I am definitely looking forward to tomorrow, Louis." I felt that somehow the budding relationship was taking a step backward. I was determined to end tonight moving forward. "Would you like to come in? I could really use some help. You know, these shoes, they are really not meant for dancing and, well, my feet are hurting. Would you mind trying to make them feel better?"

"That will be fine, Barb. I appreciated your choice of heels tonight and the sacrifices you may have made to wear them. They brought out the best in your fantastic legs. And they really did display your your pretty feet well." He caressed my right leg with the back of his hand and furtively glanced at my feet.

I sensed a thaw. "I didn't realize you found my feet pretty, dear. Do you have a little foot and shoe fetish? Tell me what you like about them, sweetie," I teased. I sat down on the bed, crossed my right leg, and began to touch my right foot.

"I prefer to think of it as an admiration." Louis kneeled on the floor, gripping my knees and staring downwards. "The thin spike heels just scream of sex, Barb, how else am I supposed to think about them? I admire the way the ankle straps of your sandals draw me into the exquisite features of your delicate ankles ... " I caressed my right ankle. "... and how the sole design shows off your very high arches ..." I then caressed my arch. "... and how the thin front strap just highlights and exposes your beautiful toes, so well-manicured, so absolutely cute dangling a bit over your platforms, so succulent, so inviting ..." Louis seemed to be going into a trance now, obviously associating my shoes and feet with sexual urges.

"You know, my toes are a little cold right now." I wiggled my right toes. "They could use some warming up," I whispered invitingly.

Louis didn't need more encouragement to take the bait. He instantly grabbed my right sandal with both hands and placed my right big toe in his mouth. His tongue greedily licked all around it. After about a minute, he released it with a soft kiss at the end and proceeded to move onto the adjacent toe. I watched him as he did this for each toe on my right foot. Louis looked up at this point, expectantly. I nodded, reading his thoughts.

He immediately dropped to his head further, while grabbing my left sandal and lifting my entire left leg up, so that he could resume on my left toes. I wasn't sure if I wasn't becoming more aroused than he evidently was. I was witnessing this powerful man groveling at my feet, hungry to devour them. I closed my eyes as he started with my left big toe. I stayed in the moment, feeling the moistness of his mouth suck and lick the remaining toes and sensing my pussy leaking again.

He finished with my toes and then pushed my torso from an upright seated position to a supine position upon the bed. Still kneeling, he swung both my legs onto the bed and began kissing and licking my ankles. I couldn't take it anymore and I brought my right hand over to rub my clit. After a bit, I started gasping, making small mewing sounds. I shuddered, a small orgasm sweeping over me. In crazy desperation, I used my other hand to untie the halter of my dress, pushed aside the cups hiding my areola, and commenced rubbing my right nipple.

Louis noticed. With my remaining rational brain cells, I recognized a look I had seen many times before. He was absolutely lusting over my large pillowy-soft tits, which were now shaking and heaving with my rapid gasps. With a crazed desperation equal to mine, he panted, "I need your body now, Barb. I really, really need it. Please give it to me ..."

I just nodded with small quick head movements, eyes and mouth wide open, fingers still rubbing my clit, as I yelled, "I'M CUMINNNNNNG! Oh my God, oh my God ..."

Chapter 4

Louis then quickly launched his head from my feet to my left breast, cupping the mound with both hands, attacking the nipple with his lips, his saliva dripping all over the mammary. At this point, my legs had come together and he ground his crotch against them, apparently trying to find something to stimulate his stiffy. In the dying moments of my orgasm, I unbuckled his pants, opened the fly and pushed the garment to his knees.

I stroked his manhood as best I could with my right hand and tried to stabilize his body by wrapping my left arm around his back, but he continued to wildly grind his hips against me. When my left breast became extremely slippery from saliva, he switched over to sucking and slurping the right nipple, while continuing to fondle the left breast.

My right hand could feel pre-cum starting to drip from his penis. With the extra lubrication, my stroking became more regular. I slowly went up and down the entire shaft with my hand. Louis stopped moving his hips, his manhood sufficiently stimulated. I responded by gripping the head and rubbing his head rhythmically with my thumb, resulting in a notable twitching of his legs. He continued to play with my boobs, eventually smearing copious amounts of saliva over the surface of both of them.

Louis suddenly twisted away from my grip. He moved himself toward my head and went from prone on my body to straddling his legs around my abdomen. He placed his iron-hard rod between my tits and pushed them together. I quickly understood and replaced his hands with mine, while he placed his hands on the bed, next to my head. He spasmodically rocked his hips a couple of times. Groaning, he ejaculated thick white streams of cum, hitting and dribbling off my forehead, my mouth, my chin, my neck. He was probably spent, but I continued to encourage him to fuck my tits. "Baby, give me some more, give your lover some more ..." After jerking himself off between my chest pillows a few more times, he collapsed onto me.

It was a nice feeling having him on top of me. I managed to slide upward a bit.

While Louis lay exhausted on me, I gave him soft kisses all around his face. After a bit, Louis stirred. He returned my kisses, softly, one for one, and, in due course, we finally settled on a prolonged kiss on the lips, our tongues dancing and our arms wrapped around each other. It was my first prolonged post-sex embrace with him, one that I have never forgotten even to this day. My endorphins were running high and I was in heaven.

I unclinched first. "Louis, dear, may I sleep with you tonight? I really need to. Please, honey, I desperately need to be next to you, to feel you, to see you, to hear you," I whispered, inches from his face, locking in on his eyes.

"Of course. I would like that, too. I am so fond of you, Barb. Not just your sexy body. You. All of you. You should know that, Barb."

"Thank you," I murmured, casting my eyes downward.

"Barb, I don't think 'thank you' is the right response, but you're welcome. Now, how long will you need before you meet me in the master bedroom?" He rolled off my body, still lying on the bed.

"About an hour, maybe? It'll be worth the wait. I'll make sure that you find me pleasing, my sweetie. Oh, and one other thing ..." I got off the bed and, smiling at Louis, pulled my dress down to my feet. I leisurely walked around the room, pretending to tidy things up, nude in heels, careful to place one foot directly in front of the other, in order to maximize the wiggle of my ass and the jiggle in my boobs. I bent over a couple times, legs straight, pretending to pick up some stray lint, my ass and sex directly pointing at him each time. Then I walked into the bathroom.

I quickly showered, leaving the semen-encrusted choker on, and washed my face. The sticky cum on my upper body, as well as my own sticky juices around my inner thighs, were washed off. I brushed my teeth and gargled with mouthwash. I dried off the choker. I spritzed a bit of perfume on my neck, behind my ears, and on my wrists.

I put on a matching lingerie set. I had done a photo shoot about a year ago with this exact set and the company had let me keep it. I had been waiting for the right time to wear it and now was the right time. The outfit was pale pink and sheer, hiding nothing.

The first piece was a lace baby doll with a hem to just above my crotch and held up by thin shoulder straps, designed with a deep V-neck, a thin satin under bust strap accented with a long central bow, and a flyaway back. I was proud how my full and firm boobs remained high on my chest, despite being unsupported, and how well the cups of the baby doll highlighted my areolas and enticingly prominent nipples. The second piece was a lace garter that narrowed in the back to afford a full view of the entirety of my toned round butt. I placed a crotchless pair of panties, which consisted of a mesh front panel that just barely covered over my tiny landing strip and floss-thin material everywhere else. The panties required much patience to put on appropriately, as they were secured to the hips by delicate ties on each side, in order to facilitate removal. I giggled at how much time it had taken to tie on the piece, knowing how quickly it would fall off. I then rolled up a back-seamed lace-top stocking up each leg. As I fastened each garter strap, I couldn't help but think how smooth the stockings felt on me.

The final piece of the set was a floor-length sheer silk gown, with wide long butterfly sleeves, white trim, and a thin white silk front tie.

I saw my reflection in the full-length mirror. I knew the effect of the ensemble would be devastating. The pretty lingerie set, while pretending to defend my innocence and modesty, was essentially a transparent wrapping that seductively brought attention to and inviting inspection of each part of my young, supple, flawless body. The whole thing was a like fantasy bridal set, except in pink.

Excited and confident, I reapplied make-up. I decided to continue to emphasize a demure look. My hair was still in an updo and I left it alone. I lengthened my lashes with copious mascara, applied neutral eye shadow with a matte finish, and used very little eye liner. I brushed on a heavy amount of pink blush around my cheeks. I outlined my lips and applied glossy pale pink lipstick. Then I put on the choker back on and a pair of dangling single-stoned diamond earrings. Finally, I slipped on my sandals. They were a pink pair that I had spent countless hours looking for this past week, trying to find something that best matched the exact shade of pink of the lingerie set. The front of each sandal had a single set of three crisscrossing straps with a cute rose detail centrally where the straps crossed; the back of the sandal was a simple yet graceful unbuckled slingback; the sole was flat to the ground and the stiletto heel was only 3 inches in height. I grinned, sure that Louis would have plenty to "admire" with my choice of footwear. It oozed sensuality and showed off my delicate ankles, high arches, and succulent toes to full effect, while keeping my standing height such that I would not tower over him in my attempt to convey a submissive role.

I exited the guestroom and crossed past the dining and living rooms to arrive at the master bedroom. I knocked on the half-closed door. "May I come in?"

"Just wait." Through the crack in the door, I watched Louis get off the fully made bed, walk to the other side to fold over the near corner of the top sheets of the bed, and dim the lights. He was dressed just in a black silk boxer short. Despite already having had two orgasms each, I had not seen his nearly naked body. I was not disappointed. He had large and defined muscles everywhere, with very little excess fat. He had impressively large pecs and arms, a narrow waist with a hint of a six-pack abdomen, and thick thighs. I was going to enjoy being nude in bed with him, touching and being securely held by that magnificent physique. My pussy was already becoming wet in anticipation.

I entered and he gasped sharply. I decided to play out the moment, to establish my submissive role. I cast my head and eyes slightly downward and asked, "Do I please you, sweetie? Am I pretty enough for you to sleep next to you in bed tonight, honey?"

Louis circled behind me. He wrapped his muscular arms around my waist and whispered in my ear, "You look so divinely beautiful, Miss Wilder. It would be my pleasure to share my bed with you tonight. Would you consider sleeping with me nude, though? It would be much more intimate, don't you agree?"

Still facing away from him, I softly replied, "Would you like to undress me, sweetie? I would prefer that you unwrap your present yourself. Be gentle, please. I am feeling quite vulnerable." That last phrase came out of my mouth as a line for the role I was trying to project, But as I heard it spoken, I realized it was true. I actually was feeling vulnerable, with this powerful man starting to peel away not just my lingerie, but also my emotional defenses.

"Barb, please trust me. I will be gentle with you. Your heart is safe with me. I will worship you."

Hearing this, my pussy started to leak yet again tonight.

"Naughty girl. I can see all of you inside the exquisite wrapping of yours." Louis untied the gown and slipped it off my shoulders. As the gown floated down to the white carpet, he tenderly kissed my neck a couple times before working his kisses down my back and kneeling. I moaned quietly. He deftly untied the side straps of my wet knickers, which, in its dampness, dropped quickly between my feet. He moved away. "Turn around and step forward a little," he commanded.

I complied. He had positioned himself about two meters away, eyeing me yearningly. "Your sex is so pretty, Barb, so well-manicured, the lips so sensual and inviting. May I enter inside tonight?"

"I'm so wet down there ..." I knew it was a silly reply to blurt out, but my mind was fogging up with lust and I could only come up with that primal response. I could feel liquid oozing down my thighs.

Louis unhurriedly advanced toward me. His strong arms encircled my waist from the front and he gave me a soft kiss on my lips. "Patience, patience, my dear," he murmured. He then untied the back of the babydoll and pushed the straps off my shoulders. The piece floated to the floor. I was now just wearing only a garter belt, stockings, and sandals.

Louis stepped back again. "Your figure is so perfect, Barb. I'll bet you are so proud to possess such large and firm breasts ... and with such nice long and erect nipples to boot. And your tummy, so flat and defined. Barb, I would like to ask a favor. Will you press your bosom against me tonight? Will you let me explore the curves of your belly tonight?" I could only manage to make an unintelligible squeak. "I would like you to remove your belt now," he ordered. Almost mad by carnal passion, I fumbled to unclip the thin satin garters from the stockings and to unfasten the belt; the piece pooled on the ground next to the babydoll. "Now look at me and stand up straight," he directed. I gazed back at Louis, fully erect, slightly pigeon-toed, knees nearly touching, arms a bit behind my sides.

I was in a vulnerable pose and was indeed was feeling truly vulnerable. I was so deranged by an unrequited sexual frenzy that I had lost control of all my voluntary thoughts and movements. What I had intended as an act had turned into real submission to Louis.

"How considerate, Miss Wilder, you have left me with the opportunity to carefully inspect your legs and feet. You know how much I admire them ... and your delicate sandals, I find them so very sensual." He paused for a moment, just staring at me and now rubbing the bulge underneath his shorts. After a while, he continued, "Please lie back on that black leather chair over there. And spread your legs wide."

I did as he asked, stumbling and almost unconscious, as my brain was now a dense haze of fear and desire. After staring at my moaning and wanton form for a minute, Louis drew toward me and kneeled. He wrapped his hands around my ankles and buried his head in my crotch, his tongue alternating on my uncovered upper thighs, licking off the juices. My pussy now felt as if it was pouring out like a faucet and he responded by lapping up my slit over and over. At the top of each slurp, he pressed his tongue against my clit, each time eliciting a loud whimper that pierced through my otherwise non-stop moaning. He continued at this for an agonizing amount of time and I was starting to pass out. Just before I would have passed out, his lips locked in on my clit, sucking it hard while simultaneously inserting fingers inside me. I shuddered violently, felt a painful wave of pleasure, shrieked, and then went blank.

When I awoke, my stockings were off and I was lying sideways across the wide arms of the leather chair. Louis was smiling at me five feet away on his huge bed, lying nude halfway inside its sheets. "Would you like to come to bed now, Barb?"

I nodded and swung myself off the chair. I stood up, my sandals still apparently on. I slowly moved over toward the bed, knowing Louis was getting off on watching my naked body teetering in my sexy heels. Before I could lie down, Louis asked, "Could you take down your hair? I want to see you in your full glory."

"Anything, my dear," I replied. It took me over a minute to remove all the pins holding my updo in place. I shook my head and my long, voluminous hair draped over my entire upper body. I swept it back, uncovering a pleading smile directed at Louis. "Make love to me now, sweetie."

Louis motioned me to lie down and I did. He rolled me onto my back, between the warm and slippery satin sheets. Slowly and gently, his manhood penetrated me. His rock-hard penis felt so good and so natural inside me. It filled me up, both physically and spiritually. There was nothing to say. We gazed at each other, as he patiently went in and out of my sex, pausing every few strokes to tenderly kiss different parts my smiling face. After about fifteen minutes of mutual bliss, he whispered, "May I cum?"

I nodded adoringly. He thrust more quickly and I felt my pussy flooded. His eyes looked down at mine lovingly and I responded in kind. We embraced intimately, kissing deeply until his penis softened.

He pulled out and much of his seed spilled out onto the sheets. Neither one of us cared. I turned slightly to my right side, lying on some wetness. Louis did the same, his right arm under my neck and his left arm draped over the two large mounds on my chest.

He was tenderly spooning me and we dozed off in that position. I am so happy I have him all to myself. I felt fulfilled.

THE END

Description

Maria made a deal with a vampire who posed as a young man called Leonardo. She was supposed to give up her daughter when she got to the age of thirty-five to become his wife. Along the way, she changed her mind and allowed her daughter, Rosetta, to date whoever she wanted.

Strangely, all the men who declared interest in her ended up mysteriously dying. Maria and her husband, Antonio, eventually got tired and decided to help their daughter in the search of a husband. It didn't take long since their family friend and business partner, Lorenzo, had a son who had married a non-Mexican and was planning to divorce her.

A chance presented itself before them. Lorenzo's son, Eduardo, was asked to marry Rosetta and maintain the family business. But all those plans came crumbling down as Leonardo came back for Rosetta just as agreed. She was his and no one could take her away from him!

Chapter 1

"Will you marry me Rosetta and make me the happiest man in the world?" he posed the long-awaited question.

It was a moment of silence as people waited anxiously to witness the couple make their vows. Everyone moved closer, with profound feelings of disquiet. It all came to a standstill as hope engulfed through Eduardo's feet. He was so excited to hear her say yes!

Unlike Eduardo, Rosetta was swimming in a river of doubt. There was fear that erupted from deep within her that made her lose her focus. She had desired such a moment for a long time but not with Eduardo. She felt like she was just a victim of circumstances, and there was no way she could change that.

She remained silent and seemed carried away for a moment. Her eyes were glued to the clouds as if looking for answers to something totally unrelated to Eduardo. Everything around her suddenly changed. The guests were filled with confusion as they stared at each other with funny guesses and weird glances.

The party then turned gloomy and so did the groom. The bride to be feigned a smile as the weather disapproved of her actions. Loud claps of thunder filled the space as if trying to retaliate for the emotional damage that was about to go down. The sudden changes in the weather made it even harder for the invited guests to blend as they all quickly went back to the hall. It was going to rain soon and the party was also going to end! Probably or possibly!

Eduardo remained on his knees still waiting for her response. He wore his usual broad smile. He had to give her time to answer his question. There was no need to jump to conclusions and assume she didn't want to marry him because according to him, she wanted that! She had told him.

Eduardo had a great smile. It was something that made it easier for him to put coworkers and clients at ease. It helped him make good relations even in the corporate world as he got clients with his personality. And now, even with all the bad signs staring ruthlessly at him, he believed Rosetta was in love with him and would certainly say yes to his marriage proposal. He maintained his cool.

Deep inside, he was filled with gratitude. Eduardo could not believe that it was all coming to pass. Thoughts of how their life would be as a couple crowded his mind. He was ready to grant her biggest wishes. He wanted to give her the exact wedding of her dreams. Make her feel like a queen that she was—just anything and everything for her to be happy. He could not help but picture himself sleeping next to her cuddling with her and waking up to see her beautiful face every morning. She was going to be his sunshine and there was no doubt about that. It was going to be the best experience in his life. Sadly, it was not the same for Rosetta.

Rosetta had a different mindset. Her reasoning did not match the guests. While many saw the engagement as a love bond, she saw it clearly as a business deal. Protection of business interests from both families. A reality that none of her family members wanted to admit.

Rosetta wanted a relationship that would grow from mere attraction to a strong bond. A beautiful feeling that would make her sleepless, stimulated by a touch from someone she loved. She would be so proud talking about their first meeting, how life had been since their first encounter.

Sadly, the man could offer that was Leonardo, and thinking about their last meeting only made her hate herself. She was in love with him, yet she had asked him to keep away since the marriage had already been set by both families. There was no turning back. Leonardo did not leave without giving her something to think about.

"I said you have to go! My engagement party is tomorrow. This can't work! And you need to stop visiting!" She had told him the previous night. He prepared to leave but he had something to say before he did. Rosetta looked out into the darkness as the shadow before her claiming to be Leonardo spoke. She had never seen his face as he always visited at night and never allowed her to see him. According to Rosetta, he was a strange man. Maybe if he were posing like a real human, all the weirdness would come to an end.

"I don't dispute that. Everything is set So what. Is that what you want? Because if it is, I'll stop bothering you. I'll let you be!" Leonardo had questions. He knew that she did not love Eduardo and was only with him because of her father. He also knew that she was madly in love with him. She was just scared. Little did he know that the questions he was asking opened her eyes...

"Maybe, you have a point. The problem is how do I dump a real man...I mean a man who has a face for a faceless man like you! Who are you anyway?" she was tired of his innuendos. If he really wanted them to have a real relationship then he had to show his face!

"I understand. You're scared of saying no to Eduardo and then coming back to your lonely bed?" He was moved by her words. He came closer and held her hands rubbing them smoothly.

"One day I'll visit you. It could be tomorrow. I don't know. But what I know for sure is that I'll show you my face, and I will definitely take you home with me. There will be no engagement, none of all that. I'll take you with me wherever I go. You are the love of my life and I know you love me too....and so you know, it might be sooner than you think." And with that, he left.

Rosetta loved Leonardo no matter who he was. Even though he was behaving weird, she felt she could live with that. There was something so strong about him that made it harder to stay apart. Every night Leonardo visited at wee hours, and would find her waiting for him. She dressed up and looked good for him way before he came. Even though she never saw his real face, it was not the same for him. He claimed that he could see her clearly even in the dark.

Rosetta started looking at Eduardo in a different perspective. She realized that she was making a huge mistake by marrying someone she didn't love just because she wanted to impress her parents. And after Leonardo left, she couldn't sleep. She spent hours turning and crying as she waited for dawn to rise.

The look on her father's face in the morning made all her efforts to pull out of the marriage plans futile. She lost the hope she had the night before when Leonardo visited. Hopelessness took charge and there was no way out of it.

There was something not adding up about her mother. She had started withdrawing away from the planned marriage but she could not show it openly. Two days ago, she had asked her daughter to forgive her. She couldn't go against her husband. It made Rosetta understand that her mother was not for the idea but was playing along.

Mixed emotions made it harder for her. A part of her wanted to say yes and make her daddy proud but her heart was saying no. It constantly reminded her that she had strong feelings for someone else. She wanted to opt out but wait. Her father's wrath would certainly bring her down. She was not supposed to question him. It was disrespectful.

"Will you marry me, sweetheart?" Eduardo repeated his question. Rosetta was shocked and almost jumped out of her shoes. She had forgotten about the engagement. There was something troubling about Eduardo. His tone had suddenly changed and he was almost losing it. He was demanding and was displaying anger toward her. He had noticed the recent change in her but he was not going to face his family in shame again—not after divorcing his wife. It had to work by all means!

All was going on smoothly, until a middle-aged man walked in. She was about to say "yes" but instead she let out a whisper. Nobody heard it as it was not loud enough. She couldn't get her eyes of him. He was smartly dressed in the same clothes as Eduardo.

They were both dressed in black and but the new man had a beard and long hair. He went straight to Rosetta and then smiled at her. He then stretched his hand and shook hers, then took his seat. Nobody understood what was going on. After the young man took his seat, Rosetta followed him, leaving Eduardo on his knees holding a ring.

Something needed to be done since Eduardo was mad. Eduardo stood up angrily and went to get his woman who was already in the new man's arms. He was about to punch him when Maria walked in. She had gone to the washroom and didn't see the new man walk in.

It was Leonardo!

Chapter 2

"Leonardo! Leonardo!" she shouted. Everyone turned to look at her. They thought she was sick but she wasn't. Maria knew exactly what was going on. Leonardo had been forced to come after she refused to honor her end of bargain. It was not business as usual!

"Please I beg you, don't hurt her. She's a good woman Leonardo, please don't hurt her!" She was crying. The guests exchanged glances wondering what was going on.

"I know she is Maria. Don't you worry. She is our princess! How could I forget that?" He was laughing hysterically. Rosetta's father decided to defuse the situation. He came and took his wife away but she continued screaming at the top of her voice as they left.

"He's going to kill all of us! You should let him marry Rosetta!" She left the hall and immediately after, Rosetta could not hide her joy. The kind of warmth she felt in his arms was heavenly. He looked more handsome than she had thought. She needed to be with him. She clung to his hands as he made her feel at peace with herself.

All that time, Eduardo was in rage. He could not believe that Rosetta had walked away from him. She acted like he meant nothing to her, treating him like he didn't matter. It cut him deep. He looked at the wedding ring he had bought for her only to be turned down. He tried to hit Leonardo but he was too strong for him. He held Eduardo's hand and broke it. Leonardo then lifted him up and threw him through the window. He was so wild and was roaring like an animal. When the guests saw that, they started running and within no time, the hall was empty. Not even Eduardo's father remained. He had to run for his life!

***

Six Months Ago

There was a lot going on in Rosetta's family. Her father wanted her to start a family of her own citing that most of the women her age have married and settled down. She begged him to listen to her but he said they had better plans for her. He was planning to get her a husband in two weeks or so! Little did he know, it was going to result to more pain than healing his daughter's broken heart.

Time moved quickly. Antonio brought the news just as he had promised. Her father informed her that he had arranged for her to meet her husband to be and that she is required to be at the introduction.

"I can get a man of my own. What is it so hard to understand Mama?" she had told her mother after her father left the room. She felt insulted.

"Sorry Rosetta, but we can't go against your father. Please get ready!" she said and left. Rosetta couldn't understand why they were deciding for her. Still, she didn't want to fight anymore. She had run out of options and so, she had to do as advised by her parents. After all, they said they meant well for her.

Rosetta had been matched before but she had not found anyone worth settling down with. She felt like they were just wasting her time. Finally, she got tired of the dating games and explored other options. And in her quest for true love, she went to a dating site and came up with an impressive profile. It caught many suitors' attention but she kept ignoring them. Until the day she came across Leonardo's profile. She could not help but notice the great photos he had shared.

"Ooh he looks so handsome!" Rosetta noticed. She zoomed in on the photo that was right before her eyes. She almost kissed her phone screen. She went through the many photos popping up slowly and very keenly. She could not help but wish she had someone just like him.

Rosetta was quick to notice that indeed, Leonardo had a great sense of fashion. Everything about him was trendy and classy. There were also other photos of him in a very big office and scrolling down the profile, she came across a company he managed. She promised herself she would visit the company one day and request to see him. But, she felt that it would make her look needy. Everything fell into place when he initiated a conversation through a chatroom. The messages kept coming and she gave in to his flow.

A few days later, they were both head over heels in love with each other. Their conversation was flowing perfectly and most of their likes and dislikes seemed the same. They had so many things in common. Their favorite meals, their dressing choices, and even their religious beliefs. They were both Catholics. The similarities were a good sign but also the unending compliments from Leonardo made him stand out from all her exes. He kept telling her that she was beautiful and he also loved seeing her in a dress.

And as usual, all was going well. She was getting ready for the visitors just as asked when more texts popped up. She had to sit down and reply. They were beautiful lines with the same magic touch as they always had. She didn't even hear her father walk in. She was carried away by the nice words coming from Leonardo. They continued to message each other.

"Please send me more photos of you in a dress. I just want to look at you today sweetheart. You are all I think about these days. You are the true definition of a beautiful woman," he texted. Rosetta read the text message and blushed.

"I'll send you one in a bit…" She was not sure which one of her photos to send. She went through her gallery and picked several. She then pressed the send button. Leonardo was so excited. Her father saw the message thread as he stood right behind her. He was disappointed in her. Still, he didn't talk to her so she continued to text since she didn't know he was there.

Ever since she was young, Rosetta always had self-esteem issues. She doubted her worth until that day Leonardo contacted her. He boosted her self-esteem in mysterious ways through compliments and shows of affection. He liked her and was ready to love her if given a chance.

To Rosetta, it was immense. She couldn't explain it but she could feel that there was something special about Leonardo. Other than the attractive face and muscles portrayed in his photos, he had quite an interesting personality.

He was also very different from all the other guys she had dated in the past. His sounded sincere and every word that he told her kept ringing in her mind. The way he said it, through messaging and calling. It unleashed a fire in her, so strong that she felt everything else come to a standstill. She was in a world of her own, a place where all things were perfect.

With time, her nights became warmer and calmer as she held her pillow thinking of him. An imaginary man who had the powers to keep her awake. It was a dream come true. If only she was sure about Leonardo but then, it was still too early to tell how serious he was. She imagined all the great times they would create together. She prayed and waited for a miracle to happen and bring him by her side before they took her to Eduardo.

Leonardo was a rare species. He made it known to her as soon as he started messaging her that he admired her. He expressed his innermost feelings and confessed to her how happy he would be if she loved him back. He wanted a chance to make her the most loved person in the world. And those words swept her off her feet. She was without a doubt the most important person in his life.

As their conversation continued, their bond grew stronger. He spoke about his life and even confided in her about many things. He mentioned that he didn't have parents that they were killed when he was young and he grew up in an orphanage. He was never lucky enough to get foster parents and his childhood was a struggle. The words created a bond between them. Rosetta felt sorry for him. She wanted to be a shoulder for him to lean on.

Well, Leonardo got what he wanted from her, total sympathy and attention.

Chapter 3

Within a few weeks of messaging, he was requesting for a face to face meeting. *How nice of him to ask,* Rosetta thought. Rosetta felt a deep connection between her and Leonardo.

It was coming true! Her prince charming was about to show up. Everyone who had thought she would never find true love was about to get a shock of a lifetime. They were all about to be put to shame more so her two younger sisters who had already gotten married and hurled all kinds of insults at her. It was time to prove to them that she was lovable. That someone as good-looking as Leonardo had noticed her. All that time, she had long forgotten about the expected visitors!

She stared at her phone in disbelief! Finally, a man was asking to meet her. She couldn't turn down such an offer. But just as she was about to type a yes to his request, someone tapped her shoulders. It was her father.

He looked at her full of disappointment. He had been there long enough and had seen the message thread. He wondered just how she could even be contemplating meeting a total stranger. Mr. Antonio felt heartbroken.

Three weeks ago, Mr. Antonio visited Mr. Lorenzo. They had planned on having a drink and discussing a few things regarding work. They owned a company together that dealt with auditing and basic accounting. They had been successful in the past few years and were very happy to see their success, but their discussion changed immediately after Eduardo came.

It was not like him to visit his parents unannounced. Worst of all, on a weekday. But what he wanted to discuss was urgent. It could not wait even a day. He had been going through a lot and even though, he was hurting, he had kept it from his family members for a long time. It was finally the best time to put everything out in the open.

There were wrangles in his marriage recently and he felt that they were taking a toll on him. His marriage was on the verge of breaking up. He wanted to file for divorce but he needed parental guidance, so he came to ask his parent's house for advice straight home from the office. It was a burning issue and he couldn't hold onto it anymore.

"It's okay son, you can talk to me in Antonio's presence. He is like family," suggested Lorenzo on seeing the discomfort written all over his son's face when he found Antonio seated across the table. But Antonio was ready to leave. He spoke.

"If it's a problem, and you need privacy it's okay, I can just leave," he said trying to ease the already rising tension among them but Lorenzo insisted that he stayed.

Eduardo explained everything that was going on. He didn't feel the spark anymore. He felt distant and his efforts to change or even address things were going unnoticed. Well, his parents never liked his wife. His mother claimed that she wasn't even Mexican and didn't even know how to cook Mexican dishes!

Every time they visited, her mother would spend the first sixty minutes complaining that her son was poorly fed. That he looked malnourished. She would rush to the kitchen and prepare Mexican dishes and then sit across admiring her son eating. She made Eduardo's wife, Elizabeth feel like she had failed.

Eduardo's parents didn't see the need to fight for the marriage. Their advice came as a shock to him. But on the other hand Antonio seemed to enjoy the advice they were offering. He brightened up when his friend, Lorenzo suggested that their son should look for a true Mexican. Someone with a strong background and more similarities than differences. And with that said, Mr. Antonio had a brilliant idea.

His idea was not the best but it was applauded by Lorenzo too. It would help in the company management generally as they had fifty-fifty ownership. And so they set up a meeting for the two young ones. The arrangement was treated like an emergency. They had to set the record straight and remove Eduardo's wife from the picture. After all, they had no child to tie Eduardo with child support. Eduardo was in for the idea.

Finally, the day came, and instead of Rosetta getting ready as requested, she had locked herself in her room going through Leonardo's profile and messaging him. Her father managed to twist the doorknob. He wanted to have a word with her as he had noticed that she wasn't taking the visit seriously. When he saw her sending photos to a stranger he could not hide his anger!

"Do you realize that we are doing this for you Rosetta?" he asked. His angry voice went through the walls and her mother came in. Maria observed her daughter keenly and chose not to speak. Rosetta sat there in silence. She felt that there was no need to explain anything to her parents. After all, they had decided to play matchmaker. They didn't even care about her feelings.

"Rosetta! Get up right now, go to the bathroom and freshen up. Apply something on your face. You need to look good for Eduardo to notice. You need to impress him." He meant it.

"Please go sweetheart. We all want the best for you baby girl," her mother said. Her father then left, leaving Maria behind. Rosetta turned and stared at her mother with resentment. She spoke...

"If you really wanted the best for me as you say, you should have allowed me to decide who I wanted to marry," but her words fell on deaf ears. Maria ignored her. She had no choice but clean up and join the rest of the family for dinner downstairs.

Leonardo continued texting. It was like he knew something was going on. Rosetta held her phone tightly, pressing it against her hand. A strong desire to meet Leonardo was starting to push her to extreme limits. Her father wanted her to get married to Eduardo while she wanted to try out her luck with Leonardo.

They waited for the guests to arrive as Maria kept smiling to herself. She was happy that finally, her first-born daughter was going to get a better match. Maria remembered the three exes her daughter had brought home back then. They looked so happy together and then boom, the relationships ended and the suitors disappeared. Maybe it was time to get involved in her dating life. They could help, maybe!

Finally, Lorenzo came accompanied by his wife and son. They were welcomed and food was served. They talked about a lot of things and at some point, the parents asked the children to give them some time. They wanted them to mingle, to learn about each other.

Rosetta stood up and took her phone with her. She had three unanswered texts from Leonardo. He wanted to know if she was ready for a meeting. She told him she was not ready to meet him yet but would love to in the near future. Rosetta wanted the matchmaking storm to calm down before they met. Leonardo didn't fight it. He totally understood that the right time would come and she would indeed come through.

When Rosetta and Eduardo came outside, each and every one took their own seats. They sat facing different sides. Rosetta was glued to her phone chatting with Leonardo as Eduardo closed his eyes in deep thoughts. He wanted to start a conversation but Rosetta wasn't interested. Still, he tried his luck to woo her.

"Do you believe in arranged marriages, Rosetta?" he asked. Rosetta feigned a smile.

"No, it's a total waste of time. I would rather live alone than have an arranged marriage," she said sarcastically.

"Then what are you doing here?" he wondered.

"The same as you, passing time." She was damn serious.

"Wait what, my marriage failed because I always choose bad girls., I want my parents to choose for me a life partner, and maybe it would work this time around." It sounded stupid to Rosetta.

"You think so?" she asked. It hit him so hard that he was stunned. He doubted himself and even questioned his sanity. Maybe Rosetta had a point, maybe it was too soon to move on.

Chapter 4

It was not easy for Eduardo, He thought he could easily dump Elizabeth and move on but his misery was evident even after the visit.

He sank down as he remembered the good times he had with his wife. They were great times indeed. To his surprise, he felt if life ever allowed him, again. He would gladly create more memories with her. He still missed her.

Like any other couple, they had had their own share of ups and downs. But it wasn't enough reason to walk away. His parents thought otherwise though after listening to his complaints.

The once strong love was affected by the many arguments that didn't end well. Initially, Eduardo thought it wise living apart for some time, terming it as a temporary separation or rather a break of some kind to put things between them in perfect order. But instead, Rosetta was brought in the limelight by his parents immediately after he moved to his parents' house. His move only worsened the storm between them. Things were never going to be the same again, not when his parents hated his woman. They advised him to try out someone else.

Later that day, after the guests left. Rosetta's family retired to bed earlier than usual. They had discussed a lot of things and each of them needed time to process. Rosetta's parents saw the idea as an amazing one. It would strengthen the bond they had with Lorenzo's family.

Strangely, Maria had a visitor in her sleep. It was Leonardo...and no, it was not just a dream. Leonardo was there in her bedroom!

"Hello Maria..." said Leonardo. He was sitting on one side of the bed comfortably counting the stars from where he was seated. The bedroom window was wide open as a soothing breeze filled the room. She pulled the duvet and covered her husband's legs. Then turned to Leonardo.

"You need to leave. My husband is going to wake up and you'll bring me more problems Leonardo," she said tensely.

"Not today dear. We made a deal and you are trying to ghost me! In case you forgot, I am not human so if you continue to ghost me, I will be a real ghost I assure you!" There was an uproar in the room as the windows crashed. Still, he was seated unmoved. Antonio woke up. Maria tried to push him away from the bed but he was too strong to move.

"Come on Maria, he can't see me unless I want him to," he said as he watched Antonio talk to his wife.

"Did you hear that?" he asked but Maria pretended to have been asleep.

"No, I heard nothing. Go back to sleep dear, there is nothing." she said and Antonio went back to sleep.

Maria remained awake. She was worried about her daughter. She had agreed to make a deal with a vampire since she didn't want to die. She knew Rosetta would be mad at her if she ever found out about her arrangement. But she had to as it was the only way they could leave the hospital alive. Leonardo spared them that day. After the incidence, he disappeared only to show up that night.

Maria lived her life believing that he had gone back to wherever he came from and would never come back to haunt them.

Indeed, Leonardo had been busy serving his master. He had broken so many rules in the vampire world and he was so scared of failing again. His only wish was to be with Rosetta. It was something that he had worked for since the day he saw her at the hospital. His wish was about to be granted. But not under Maria's watch. She grinned as Leonardo disappeared into the dark.

***

Earlier That Day

"The only reason I agreed to this weird arrangement was because you were loyal, and always have been. You served me from your heart and I wanted to give you what you desired most in the world. I still can't believe you chose a woman over all the things you had power over. Why Leonardo?" the master questioned but Leonardo didn't want to talk about it.

He had been with Rosetta spiritually, watching her grow and protecting her so many times without her knowledge. But he was also to blame for the many mysterious things that kept happening in Rosetta's life, including the disappearance of her ex-boyfriends. He killed them all.

Leonardo had kept his promise. He said he would physically visit when Rosetta grew up. He came to remind Maria that she could easily lose her life for working together with Antonio yet she knew where Rosetta was destined to be, and with whom.

Leonardo was a patient man and had given her enough time to mature. He then approached her on a dating site. Even though he used someone else's photos, he was sure the young lady had developed feelings for him. He could tell by the kind of distraction she had the whole afternoon during Eduardo's visit. He was sure about one thing, he was going to win her with or without anyone's help. She was his.

***

Two Days Later

Antonio called Rosetta to join them during breakfast. She did and for the first time in a long time, she looked happy. She was dressed in a long red dress and greeted by everyone.

"Morning family," she said as she took her seat.

"Ooh, you look happy today...do you mind sharing with us?" Antonio said, but Maria interrupted him by asking if he

97

needed more juice. She served them both and then sat down. She looked distant.

"Are you okay Mom?" asked Rosetta. Maria shook her hand. She lied she was fine but she wasn't, not after talking to Leonardo. Antonio turned to Rosetta.

"I hope you've thought about Eduardo, there is no turning back. A few months from now we'll be hosting your engagement party and a wedding will follow in a month's time," he said as he sipped the last drop of juice in his glass. Maria was shaken. She stammered and seemed out of place.

"We need to give them time to know each other well, to fall in love and connect without us forcing it on them. Even though they look so good together, we need to understand that they are grown-ups!" she said. Antonio could not believe what he had just heard. Since when did Maria start second-guessing him? Antonio didn't want to argue. He was actually late for work. He picked up his jacket and left. Maria knew that her daughter had questions about the whole turn around and so she left the table too. Rosetta continued to have breakfast alone.

Maria was going through a lot. She knew that she had to keep her word or lose her whole family. Rosetta was the only reason her whole family was still breathing. Maria made a promise to the devil himself after running out of options. She never shared her story with anyone until recently when Leonardo showed up in her dream. She had thought that the vampire gave up but she was wrong. It appeared that he didn't and was back with a bang, very much willing to take back what was declared his many years ago.

Chapter 5

Thirty-five Years Ago

Maria went to deliver her first born daughter Rosetta. Even though she pretended to have forgotten, there were strange things that happened and reminded her that it was not all over. It made her scared, no matter how much she wanted to share. She was warned that the consequences would be far worse. For that reason, she kept it a secret even to her husband.

Maria remembered what transpired that day. She was feeling unwell and didn't want to disturb her husband who had been very busy with work. She decided to walk to the hospital which was not very far from her house. But along the way, her condition worsened and so she fell and lost consciousness. She lay by the roadside. People thought she was sleeping but she was fighting for her life. Suddenly someone saw her and decided to help.

Deep in the forest, sat the master, they called him father. It was a cemetery that had been forgotten decades ago. The vampires' family would all come together and discuss their progress. Each and every one of them had spoken apart from Leonardo. He had been pleading with his master to be allowed to mix with humans.

"I'm tired of your whining, I want you to go there and blend with the damn humans," his voice shook the ground. The trees went down breaking and there was a storm.

"You mean it Father?" he was excited.

"Yes but I want you to take your brother with you," he went on.

"Why? You know I don't like him, Father," he argued.

"That's exactly the reason I want him to go with you. Go hunt the humans and get the woman of your dreams. I will help you trace her. She will be born today....so hurry," he said and then walked back to the woods.

"Seriously Father you didn't give me the directions, a map or something," he said angrily.

"You are a vampire, find your way." He then disappeared.

Later that day, Leonardo found himself on the other side of the hospital. He laughed hysterically as cars passed, others hitting him while some crushed trying to escape from him. He was immortal. He couldn't even bleed. He had been given a chance to come back and mingle and finally get a chance to experience love.

It had been a long time since he had something to eat. He was thirsty for blood and the first place he spotted when he woke up was the hospital. He stood up and was about to go straight to the reception but along the way he spotted Maria. Immediately, he knew there was something in her. There was a strong connection. He wanted to help her and so he did.

"Humans are so heartless. How can motorists leave a pregnant woman on the street and drive to their destinations peacefully!" he bent down and picked her up. Finally, his master was impressed, he whispered to him.

"You did good son...now your wife is going to be born in this same hospital today. The same hospital that you are going to kill people. You will watch her and make sure she is delivered safely. If you make mistakes, I will get rid of you. You will never be heard or seen.." He made himself clear.

"Okay, I hear you Father! Can you stop with all the confusion you are causing me. You will destroy me if I fail you. FINE!!' he was running out of patience. His attention was carried away by the beautiful women around him.

"Hello beautiful, you look sweet," he was acting weird. He complimented every human being he met on his way. He still had Maria in his arms curled up like a baby. They both disappeared and only reappeared in the hospital in a flash. The receptionist was moody and ignored them but Leonardo's five minutes chat with her made her get back to her senses.

"I must admit you really are very beautiful but I am not human, so your beauty is the least of my concern. This is my wife. Will you help her get the medical attention she needs. I'm not requesting you, I'm ordering you!" he said grinning his teeth, he looked scary. Deep inside, he was salivating, he was hungry and thirsty and was so tempted to kill her. The temptations were so strong that holding back was a real struggle. Then the voice of his father came back.

"I told you. You can't change who you are no matter how hard you try. Look at the thirsty you!" he laughed at him. Leonardo was out of control. The receptionist thought he was a psycho. She pretended to be friendly to save the day and took in his patient. Maria was taken to the ward as Leonardo continued on his mission. He followed the receptionist closely. He couldn't take his eyes off her. He then started killing them one after the other starting with the receptionist!

"This feels good. I can't believe I waited that long." He didn't spare anyone on the corridors. He then made his way to the hospital wards. He fed on blood and every time he killed someone he would let out a crazy laugh until he got to Maria's ward. She had just given birth to a beautiful girl called Rosetta.

Leonardo bent down to her and smiled. Maria had no idea that the man standing before her had killed everyone in the hospital and had still saved her. Still he avoided her and didn't want her to recognize him. He wore a mask that made him look like one of the doctors. He even signed her discharge papers! Maria didn't know that the same man posing like a doctor was still, the same man who had carried her and brought her in to the hospital.

Well, there was one nurse who was still alive. The one who was taking care of Maria. They both didn't know that

Leonardo had killed all of those people. They also didn't know that it was his nature to kill. He had done exactly what made him different from humans. His assignment had been to destroy as many humans as he could but Maria touched his heart. He felt sorry for her unborn child and that's why he helped her.

Looking at the little princess, there was no need to keep the nurse. She had done her work and was supposed to die like everyone else. The nurse noticed something off and wanted to inform the authorities but before she grabbed the phone, he got to her and killed her mercilessly. He laughed loudly as his body responded to the taste of human blood. All that while, his teeth remained out. His eyes turned red with every drop of blood he drank. The efforts by the police to arrest him were in vain.

The cops went on collecting bodies until they got to Maria. Nobody could believe how she had managed to survive there. When they informed her there was no one alive in the hospital, she panicked. She wanted to scream but she had no energy to do so. She wanted to go home and cool off. Suddenly a car drove to the parking lot. One of the men got out and said that he had come for his wife.

He came to the ward and assisted her with the baby. He wanted to take her home. She agreed even though she knew it was not her husband but she wanted to get out of that place. She got into the taxi and found another guy seated in the car. They were both middle-aged and were arguing about something.

"The old man only allowed you to come back here to do an assignment. Kill two hundred thousand people and go back! Simple!!" One said.

"And you think I don't know huh. I know but I want to make it right for one person. A deserving person. I will spare one. He said he would grant me my wish," said the other.

"You are not supposed to spare anyone! Humans have enjoyed this world for so long. We need to get rid of them and then have a place for us, just us! Don't you get it?" Maria was tense. She shook as the men spoke. She regretted agreeing to ride with them. It wasn't safe.

"Hey guys, I'm Maria." She spoke when she realized that they had forgotten about her. At first, she thought they were just thieves who wanted to steal and murder people but she was wrong. Their long teeth made her heart skip a bit. They were vampires!

Chapter 6

To her surprise, they didn't intend to kill her. They wanted to help her get home. Maria had many questions, she wondered why they were helping her. They didn't even know her. Her thoughts were suddenly interrupted by one of them.

"We know who you are, we are not going to hurt you...but we want a favor from..." he went on. Maria had to comply as she didn't want to lose her life. There was no point in arguing with vampires.

"Your beautiful girl, ooh she is such a cutie!" he touched her soft cheeks. Maria got back trying to prevent them from looking at her daughter. But one of them got hold of her hair and pulled her back.

"This is not a game. Do you think you are a special woman!? You aren't. I'll come for your daughter when she is fully grown. She will be my wife. And you will agree to it. That's the only way you and your handsome Antonio are going to live long enough to see tomorrow." His every word came out as a roar. She agreed but felt really sad to subject her daughter to all that.

"Before I forget, I will still look the same way I am right now. I don't grow old so don't worry, your daughter won't be marrying an older man...now get out of the car!" He made his point clear.

They dropped her home and Antonio was excited to see her. He hugged her and helped her walk to the house. He then made some tasty meals for Maria and they lived happily like they always did.

Life went back to the years when they were newly married. But even though the fling was strong between them, she could not share her story with her husband. She felt it was just a mere threat. Nothing would happen after all, how they would not even recognize her daughter when she'd be grown.

Antonio was so busy with work that he didn't even notice anything wrong about his wife.

He went on with his daily activities and worked really hard to one day get to a company's director position. Having come from a middle-class family, it encouraged him to work harder to achieve his goals.

A lot of things kept happening without him noticing. However, it came to a point where he felt Maria needed help. He thought maybe it was the kids. He researched about postpartum depression and pointed at it as the main cause of his wife's predicaments. But it wasn't. Maria kept seeing images. She would see Leonardo on the streets and run away. It was not normal to behave in such a way. The neighbors claimed she was possessed by evil spirits.

She would scream loudly in her sleep and sometimes cry uncontrollably. He would try to talk to her but she insisted she was fine. He would then watch her sleep and go off to dreamland. He admired the chubby cheeks he had fallen in love with the very first time they met. Antonio remembered everything that transpired between them that day. The heavy rains, not forgetting the crazy traffic.

He vividly remembered how he had ignored traffic rules and resulted in being stopped by the police. The conversation went on for twenty minutes as the vehicles remained stuck on the road. Those that tried to find other ways or ever tried to go on the reverse were all apprehended. Antonio begged the cops to let him go as he had an early meeting with his then company's director. The cops didn't seem to buy any of what he was saying.

Maria's brother noticed the stare his sister was giving the young man and that made him even more furious. He pushed him harder. Like any other elder brother, he was overprotective of his little sister. But the said sister was not ready to quit. Instead, Maria felt so drawn into the young lad. Since it was raining, Maria sympathized with him and offered a nice treat that was readily available by then. She displayed enormous affection and moved near the accused man and generously spread out her umbrella. Maria covered Antonio, begged her brother to let him go. He was reluctant at first but finally bent the law and gave into his sister's persuasion. Maria and Antonio fell in love and the rest became history.

A journey of true love started to blossom at a higher knot. And just like that, the beautiful cheeks she fell in love with became the one feature that her babies took after genetically, huh, really beautiful genes they were.

Looking at him years later, he still gave her butterflies. Their spark was of a rare kind. It remained just as strong as it was when they first met. The truth was, there was nothing comparable to their affection. It took a lot more effort to get to such heights. Not just rubbing shoulders and sleeping effortlessly next to each other.

They planned their life together and walked the journey together for better, for worse.

* *

Thirty-five Years Later,

Leonardo was back in their lives and was not taking a no for an answer. After his appearance at night, Maria couldn't think straight. She tried her best to convince Antonio to let their daughter decide on who she wanted to live with but Antonio wasn't listening.

"Maybe we should encourage her more...the guy you told me about, the one she was messaging. Maybe they are a good match," she kept suggesting but Antonio had his own reasons. He understood that they had to have a bond for them to blend but still argued that it was not safe for her to meet a total stranger. But one thing Antonio didn't know, Leonardo wasn't a stranger!

"Our daughter needs someone we know better, a dedicated man and business minded. Look at Eduardo, he is that man," he argued.

"Well, maybe he is but remember, he left his wife just because they had a little misunderstanding. What if he does the same thing to our daughter?" she sounded worried.

"Hmm, would you rather she dated a stranger than someone we know, Maria. What has gotten into you?" he was confused.

Time went fast and within six months Eduardo proposed to her. He had fallen in love with her but she was thinking about someone else. She was thinking about Leonardo. The more Eduardo planned the engagement, the more Leonardo frequented Rosetta's bedroom. They spent nights together and in the morning she could not understand exactly what had happened. She was afraid to share the story and so she kept it to herself.

"You said you liked my name. Did you mean it?" She would ask in her dreams while clinging to his arms like a baby. She felt safer and always wanted the dreams to keep coming. They didn't stop! They kept happening and worsened with time when she started waking up to find her pants soaked. She knew that they were not dreams but in reality someone was having intimacy with her!

In the midst of confusion, she decided to lie awake one night to see her regular visitor. She made loud snores while faking sleep. Leonardo's shadow came in as usual through the window. He walked slowly and then started to kiss her lips. She wanted to stop him but his warm hands made her yearn for more. She tried to push Leonardo's mouth away, but she couldn't. He was too strong for her.

Leonardo was worried. He didn't want her to feel like he was forcing himself on her. He wanted her to desire him. To want him and to love him. He felt he had already messed up by becoming intimate with her without her consent.

He went on kissing her and seconds later she gave in to him. She kissed him back and held him close. Leonardo kissed her neck. She struggled to speak but she couldn't find the strength. She was carried away.

"Baby," she whispered. The word woke all his emotions and he held her tightly. He removed her pink nightdress and lay there naked waiting for her alpha male.

He was more than ready. He continued kissing her and within no time, he was on her breasts. They were soft and tender. He couldn't believe it when he saw them lying before him pointing at him. Her nipples were stiff as they reacted to the caresses Leonardo was giving her. He rubbed them slowly rhythmically. She was losing her breath.

Chapter 7

He loved seeing her like this.

She had desired his touch for so long. He then licked her body from head to toe and stopped at the breast once again. It had become his favorite spot. He bite the nipples a little, and she moved her body upward. Their bodies touched as his dick became erect.

She could feel his strength, he was so strong and firm. She was also dripping wet. Her vagina wanted him more and more. She opened her legs wide open and got ready for him. Instead, he asked her to come on top and ride.

Seconds later she was in control. Leonardo was moaning so loudly. His eyes turned red and scary. He couldn't control the monster in him. He held her with all his strength and turned her over. He was on top of her and pumping her. His cock was huge and the more they fucked the more it hit the side of the vagina. She was scared but she loved his energy.

Fifteen minutes later, he was still pumping. His face suddenly started to change color. His eyes became blood-like. He increased his breathing. His hands began shaking. He wasn't cumming. Instead, his vampire self came back. He was not Leonardo. His face was bleeding and so was Rosetta's pussy. She was asking him to stop but he couldn't stop. He pumped her harder and stronger that he ended up hurting her.

When he got back to his senses, he apologized and then licked her vagina. He needed to get the blood off her. He swallowed it. Rosetta looked at him like a devil. She was scared but she could not scream.

"Are you honestly really doing that? That's blood...you bruised me. I can't even walk!" she complained.

"Sorry baby, I'll bring a lubricant tomorrow sweetheart," he said confidently but she wasn't content. She wanted answers and better still, a stop to the madness that was going on at night.

"This is not happening again. The two months you've been visiting are enough. You need to stop!" she said angrily. Instead, Leonardo was focusing on her lips in the moonlight. The windows were still opened since it was the only way he would get in the room. They could see the outside and the moon seemed to light the bedroom. It was the best feature.

"Do you really think it's easy to stop?" he asked. Rosetta answered him very fast. She said it was but Leonardo moved closer to her lips.

"I know it's not, not with the intimacy we have had over the two months. Whenever I come near you, even in a dream, you always tremble...and you think that that is easy...ha-ha, don't lie to me sweetheart!" He went on as he kissed her lips. She trembled again but stood her ground. Whatever it was, it had to stop.

"Maybe, that's what you feel. But I have come to realize that my father knows what is good for me. So I'm going to....." she was interrupted by another kiss.

"You didn't say that earlier today. You said you couldn't wait to see me!" he said. He was thinking of revealing himself to her.

"Wait, who are you?" she was confused.

"I'm your guardian angel," he said but to her it was just another lie.

"Ha ha that's what everyone says. You always sneak into my room and make love to me. I've never seen your face. Are you a ghost or something?" she asked, confused.

"I'm the guy you message.. I'm your secret admirer," he clarified things but Rosetta couldn't believe it.

"Are you some kind of a ghost because one thing I know you aren't human. I mean who fucks like that!" she laughed sarcastically and it made the pain come back. She pulled her legs back together.

"I wanted you not to attend the engagement party tomorrow. I don't want you to go," he begged her.

"Sorry but I have to. I'm tired of dating and this is the right guy for me," she had made up her mind.

"But you said you wanted us to try this. You said you loved my energy last night!" he wanted her to reconsider.

"Look, whatever I have been telling you during intimacy is pure madness. You've been sneaking in and out! And look the man on the app isn't you. He is tall and has short hair. He also doesn't have a bushy beard. You do. It's not you I know that," she said, running out of patience.

"Maybe, I used the photos because I didn't want you to get scared of me. I was only trying to impress you," he was on his knees, and suddenly someone touched the doorknob. He had to go. He kissed her and disappeared into the moonlight. He was invisible.

Her mother stood at the door wondering if indeed she was talking in her dreams like she had been doing.

"Rosetta! Rosetta!" she called but she pretended to be asleep. She wasn't and could hear her just fine but she wasn't interested in long lectures. Her mother then pulled the sheets and covered her.

"She must be talking again! This girl is something else!" she said as she walked out of the room.

Rosetta spent the rest of the night awake. She couldn't help but think of Leonardo. He was great and told her exactly what she wanted to hear. She loved his energy in bed and wished to have him lie next to her all the days of her but it was not easy considering the next day.

Morning came, she was moody and so was her mom.

"Hey baby, I miss you and I can't wait to see you," he said.

"Hmm," she was silent. Since the previous night, she was having doubts. There was a lot at stake. She had just told Eduardo she loved him. She hated breaking his heart.

Her father had been at the forefront waiting for Eduardo to visit. He had promised to engage Rosetta that day. The few months were enough for courtship. There was no need to waste more time. The wedding plans were also in progress, the only remaining thing was a date which was for Rosetta to decide.

"You love me too I know and this is going to work, trust me," he assured her but she was thinking about Leonardo.

Eduardo had them picked up and taken to the venue. She was aware that Eduardo wanted to get engaged and with her father on her case, there was no turning back. She didn't want to hurt her father. They were all excited to be there. To witness their daughter getting engaged. People had drinks as they danced to soothing Mexican music. But Maria kept hearing voices in her head.

"So you've decided to give away your daughter to someone who doesn't even love her. Isn't that selfishness?!?" Leonardo asked..

"Her father has refused to listen to me. I have no other option," Maria said, defending herself.

"So you're backing out. How foolish. I only spared you because of your daughter. You and your husband are breathing because you had to raise her. She can't get engaged to anyone else otherwise, the lucky suitor is going to die like the others," the voices went on. She left the party and went to catch some air.

"And now that you have failed to honor our deal, I'm going to get her myself. I will stop the engagement!" Maria was going crazy. Suddenly it was all quiet. The clouds gathered as people waited for Rosetta to answer.

Just as promised, Leonardo took the ring that Eduardo had bought for her and posed the question himself.

"Rosetta Antonio, will you marry me and make me the happiest man in the world sweetheart?"

"Yes!! Yes!!I will marry you!" she was so happy to finally get a man of her dreams!

THE END

www.ingramcontent.com/pod-product-compliance
Lightning Source LLC
Chambersburg PA
CBHW072102150726
47999CB00005B/1844